By the same author

Historical Fiction

The Hanging Tree
Runaway
Homestead (Runaway Series: Book Two)
Chickadee (Runaway Series: Book Three)
Providence (Runaway Series: Book Four)
Savage
The Shack on the Hill
Snow Dancer (sequel to Savage)
Where Seagulls Fly (2013 Edition)
Song of the Sea
The Shepherd of St Just

Other Fiction

Away With the Fairies (Kindle only)
The Black Rose (short stories)
The Darkness Inside
Into the Depths (Kindle only)
Into the Depths & The Liquid Room (paperback compendium edition)
The Liquid Room (Kindle only)
Minos
Quiddity (2013 Edition)
Rise of the Bloodline
Spontaneous Combustion
Synergy

Oona

By Edwin Page

Curved Brick

First published to Kindle & paperback in 2019
by Curved Brick, UK

Copyright © Edwin Page 2019

No.72

to my honey bee

with love

1

At the age of thirteen, Oona slit her master's throat. The clatter of the razor on the porch gave her a start; as if waking her from a dream. Wide eyed and filled with panic, she ran.

Bare feet bloodied, arms and legs whipped by vegetation, she went breathlessly into the east. A deluge released from low clouds washed away evidence of her passage, but the past clung to her. She blinked away rainwater, but could not blink away the memory of her murderous deed.

'I have committed the greatest sin,' she mumbled as she pushed onward; a waif consumed by a storm. 'I have committed the greatest sin.'

Oona looked to the angry sky, her dark face awash and legs becoming heavy with the effort of her flight. 'I pray for forgiveness,' she said in earnest, but the torrent from heaven did not cleanse her.

She bowed her head in guilt and shame. 'I will repent,' she swore with another upward glance, 'and if it be Your will that I pay with my life, so be it.'

Almost falling due to the growing weakness of her condition, Oona heard the baying of dogs in the distance. She regained her balance, looking back and seeing nothing through the grey curtain that hung heavy over the landscape.

Focussing on the way ahead, she was filled with thoughts of being torn apart by hounds or adorning a tree with her swinging corpse, feet twitching in the last. She fought for breath through the thickness in her throat, vision blurred by rain and fatigue.

She splashed into a stream, the waters of early spring still clinging on to winter's chill. Barely noticing, she fought against the current, the level to her thighs and soaking her pale blue housedress and white pinafore.

Scrambling out and into a strand of trees on the bank, she slipped and fell onto the thick grass. Crashing into the undergrowth gathered beneath the boughs, Oona tried to catch her breath, heart heaving in the birdcage of her chest.

She rolled onto her back, struggling for air. Eyes closed, she felt the raindrops against her face. She saw the razor in her mind's eye. It was in her hand and yet she could not comprehend that this was so. Her master sat in readiness for his morning shave as she stood behind.

Her hand suddenly drew the blade across his throat. There was a gargled sound and a spurt of blood. He grasped her wrist, the initial and painful strength of his hold soon failing as he looked back in angered shock, the light going out in his eyes.

Her lids snapped open. She turned onto her side and vomited, bile burning the back of her throat.

Spitting the last of the upheaval, she stared at a beetle balancing in the grass nearby. A drop of rain hit the blade and it bounced the bug from its place. It landed on its back upon the earth, moving its legs as it attempted to turn over.

Despite her weakened state, Oona reached out in order to right the creature. Fresh cuts and abrasions encircled her slender wrist, accompanied by older scars.

Before she could lend her aid, the beetle got to its feet. It wandered off, oblivious to her presence.

'I be as nothing,' she mumbled, tears in her eyes as she glanced at the injuries about her wrist. The harsh life

2

she had run from was still apparent and its mark would always remain.

'I cannot escape.'

Hands to her chest and remaining on her side, she drifted into a daze-like condition. Staring ahead, she barely blinked as the rainfall softened, the world about her failing to make an impression on her disturbed mind.

Oona lay hidden in the vegetation. She had no idea how much time had passed. The branches of nearby trees made no movement, the wind having died after the rain had cleared south. Dusk was thickening; silent and still.

A lone star shone above. She focussed on its cold and distant light, lifting her head slightly. 'How can I be redeemed unto You?'

The star remained without opinion.

Her head sank back, breath shallow. 'I be a sinner and must cleanse my soul,' she sighed.

The vague ghost of her words hung in the air above, as if reminding her of the truth they contained. She moved on her side with a moan and grimace.

She drew herself into a ball. Closing her red-rimmed eyes, she tried to block the cold from her mind. Sleep claimed her, offering respite from her condition.

She was woken by shivering, finding little warmth in the damp dress and pinafore. A breeze brushed the back of her neck. Night had fallen and its darkness was filled with the agitation of undergrowth.

Finding that a little strength had returned, Oona sat up, expression filled with tension as her muscles ached. She rubbed her arms, holding her knees to her chest. Her teeth chattered and each pale breath was drawn into the trees as she rocked back and forth.

The sky became inky as dawn approached, the bare trees silhouetted against its vastness. The stars began to vanish from sight, only the brightest remaining as the eastern horizon grew increasingly pale.

Oona's stomach groaned and she felt its emptiness. Birdsong arose amidst the branches and helped lift her to her feet. She took an unsteady step and then another, hands out to the sides to help with balance. Every muscle ached as she traversed the wood, moving towards the rising sun, its promise of warmth urging her on.

She broke from the woodland and came to a standstill at the edge of a clearing, young firs at its edge. A small herd of deer stood by a pool, the stag looking directly at her with ears rotated forward. Its breath issued from its nostrils as it snorted, the group of five does raising their heads from the water, droplets falling from their snouts.

Oona took a step forward and the herd broke for the far side. They bounded into the shadows, the beat of their hooves heard for a short while before giving way to the spirited morning chorus.

She stumbled to the water's edge and fell to her knees, which sank into the bank. Cupping her hands, she drank with urgency, water running down her chin.

Once she'd had her fill, Oona looked about the clearing before undressing. Carefully stepping into the pool, she crouched in its shallowness and cleaned herself. She ducked her head beneath, holding her breath. The coldness of the water numbed her cheeks and offered temporary forgetfulness as she let her mind go blank.

Her lungs unable to contain themselves any longer, she raised her head and took a vigorous breath. She kept her eyes shut, droplets running down her face from her short tight hair.

Climbing, Oona allowed a little time to dry, her skin still damp when she dressed. She looked to the trees on the far side, their growth so thick that they hid the newly risen sun. Remnants of the night lingered beneath; darkness that had yet to be chased away. She imagined the shadows as demons lurking, watching her and ready to claim her sullied soul. They would take her into the depths of hell, there to find eternal night.

She shivered and tried to dispel such thoughts. Etty's wizened and kindly face came to mind, her hair greying and eyes sparkling from amidst nests of deep wrinkles. The motherly old slave had told her not to let her imagination get the better of her on more than one occasion. One time, she'd heard noises beneath the bunkhouse in the early hours. Lying upon her cot, motionless beneath the threadbare cover, she'd pictured a terrible creature with glowing eyes scratching at the underside of the floorboards with long nails thick with the dried blood of previous victims.

Overcoming the fear that held her in place, she'd made her way over to Etty on tiptoes. In the still of the night, she'd awakened the old slave with a touch to her shoulder and the whisper of her name. After explaining the reason for the disturbance, Etty had told her it was only rats foraging for food. Taking pity on the forlorn girl, she'd pulled aside the cover. Oona had slipped in beside to find comfort and sleep, as she often did after suffering nightmares borne of her treatment by their master.

She sighed as she stood by the pool. Sadness made her eyes soulful as she thought about the elderly slave whose arms had brought the only peace she'd known at the plantation. She wished she were there, that she could find the warmth of Etty's embrace.

Feeling alone and fearful, Oona set off to the south, wishing to avoid the thick forest on the other side of the pond. She passed through the pines like an apparition, soft footfalls barely making a sound against the mat of needles. Ferns grew among scatterings of rocks, the woodland dappled by sunlight.

Seeing the trunks had thinned to the east, she changed the direction of travel. Golden rays disturbed her sight as she walked. The fragrance of the pines hung heavy in the stillness, making her thoughts indistinct and bringing a semblance calm.

The splash and burble of running water washed through the trees, becoming clearer as she continued on. The ground became increasingly rocky and she spied the glint of sunlight on ripples between the trunks.

Reaching the creek, she stood on mossy rocks and surveyed the scene. Water frothed against boulders and a large branch hung with debris was jammed between a couple by the near bank. Looking north and south along its course, she considered which direction to go, unwilling to wade across due to the swiftness of the current and unknown depth.

'The free states be to the north,' she said, making her choice and setting off carefully.

Slipping and almost falling a number of times, Oona retreated further into the trees in order to find an easier route. She kept the creek in sight as the spring sun rose into the sky, her clothes drying and skin touched with its warmth.

Her body began to tire, her stomach grumbling with growing regularity. Legs heavy and the effort of the previous day's escape starting to tell, weariness began to overcome her.

A stream emptied from the mouth of a gully ahead, waters splashing over stones. She drew up to it and looked along its passage. The sides grew in height to over four feet, the roots of trees entwined and dangling. They had been hollowed to an extent, Oona imagining the stream swollen by the thaw and wearing away the bank.

'It will do,' she mumbled.

She began up the gully, balancing on rocks and holding onto roots. Progress was slow, but she eventually reached a meander in the stream, the nearside banked with earth.

Her bare feet sank into it as she leapt from the last stone. Its coolness rose between her toes as she stood a moment, looking back and only just able to see the creek through the overhanging roots and vegetation.

She walked over to the hollow, stopping and staring into the cool shadows collected beneath. Moving aside roots which hung before her, Oona made her way into its concealment, having to duck slightly despite her lack of height. She all but fell to the ground, moving onto her side with her back to the rear, glancing at the wall of earth rising behind her.

Settling her head upon her hands, she stared out at the sunlight that hung above the waters. A multitude of mosquitoes were flying back and forth within its illumination, filled with the energy of new life.

'It may be that when I wake, I will feel the same,' she mumbled hopefully before closing her eyes and trying to find sleep.

3

Waking, Oona stretched. She grimaced with pain as her body reported its aches. Hunger followed, her stomach filled with need for sustenance.

She looked out of the hollow to find dusk once more inviting the night to reign. The sky remained clear, a chill already growing within the gully and her body responding with shivering.

Getting to her feet, her legs complaining, she moved from the shelter. Without the will or strength to move them aside, the roots brushed against her head and shoulders.

Oona walked across the muddy embankment and crouched by the water's edge. She drank and splashed her face, seeking to invigorate herself.

Her nostrils flared, catching the scent of wood smoke. She looked southwest around the meander. The vegetation along the gully swayed slightly as she wondered how far the wind could have carried the fumes.

'There could be food,' she said to herself as she considered seeking out the source, 'but I could be putting myself in harm's way.'

Her belly let out a long, low groan. She looked down, placing a hand to it. 'If I don't eat…'

Oona frowned, straightening and looking to the uneven rocks that bordered the stream beyond the embankment of mud. She didn't relish the idea of having to make her way across them and turned to the overhang, wondering if she had the strength to climb up.

'Only one way to find out,' she stated, making her way back over to the roots.

Rising on her toes, she peered over, seeing nothing but tree trunks and the gathering dark between. She grasped the thickest roots and took a breath as she readied herself for the effort.

Oona heaved and swung her legs to one side, trying to find purchase with her feet. She gritted her teeth, arms straining and right foot finding a hold in a knotted bundle of roots. Forcing her body over the high bank, she rolled away from the drop and lay recovering for a while.

Gathering herself, she got up and sniffed the air, the scent of smoke still apparent and mingling with that of the pines. Discerning the direction of its origin as best she could, she set off into the forest.

After only a hundred yards, she caught sight of a cottage through the trees. Resting in a grassy clearing interlaced with wildflowers and ferns, it was no more than a shack with a stone-built chimney stack at the near end, plumes of smoke rising into the growing darkness. A short porch adorned the south side, its gently sloping roof missing a few shingles.

She moved from trunk to trunk, trying to catch a glimpse of whoever dwelt in the humble accommodation. The shutters of the single window were ajar, but she could see no sign of the occupants from her vantage point.

Drawing up to the last pine before the cottage, she lowered herself onto her haunches, holding the rough bark as she peered from behind. A scattering of bird tables stood about the clearing, surrounding the building and a couple leaning precariously.

Her gaze was attracted by movement to the left. She watched as a large squirrel scampered towards one of the tables, its back grey and head capped in black. It leapt up, the post wobbling under its weight. It selected what appeared to be a nut and sat on the table holding it between its paws, its pale stomach touched with yellow. The creature ate with little sign of caution, only occasionally glancing about for signs of danger.

'Must feel safe,' she mumbled.

The squirrel looked over, its consumption halted as it regarded her.

A crossbow bolt pierced its body, a brief screech of death released from the creature as the impact launched it from the table. It flew through the air and landed amidst the ferns and thick grass.

Oona stared in shock. The door of the shack opened and an old man exited, his broad smile visible despite the large white beard that dominated his rounded face.

He limped over to where the squirrel had fallen, his brown britches patched at the knees and the sleeves of his pale shirt rolled to his elbows. Bending, he picked it up by the tail and nodded, saying something to himself, but the words indiscernible.

'We've got meat for the stew, Dotty,' he called, carrying it back to the cottage and vanishing from sight as he shut the door.

The shutters were closed by a woman who was considerably younger than the man, her long mousy hair without a trace of grey and face lacking the deep wrinkles. There was a brief conversation within the cottage, Oona unable to hear what was said as she remained crouched behind the tree.

She looked to the forest, the night thickening with every moment. 'A little longer,' she whispered, waiting for the darkness to conceal her presence before venturing from her hiding place.

Eventually satisfied that she could not be seen, she rose and peered around the trunk. The door and window of the cottage remained closed and she could hear the regular tap of a blade against a chopping board.

Oona warily crept from behind the pine. Making towards the nearest bird table, she kept a watchful eye on the cottage.

She reached for the pieces of flatbread resting on the wood with a scattering of nuts and oat grains. Placing them into her mouth, she chewed on their stale toughness, stomach groaning with expectation and need.

Collecting up the assortment of nuts, she held them in her hand and walked to the next table, finding the same offerings. Swallowing the last of the bread as she picked up the new, she again stuffed the pieces into her mouth.

Moving from one table to the next, she moved around to the north side of the cottage as she collected anything remotely edible. Gathering up her pinafore, she used it as a pouch, filling it as she went.

She felt at greater ease to the rear of the building. There were no windows from which she could be spied and her movements became less considered. She grasped at the foodstuff of the next table she came to, a nut rolling across the wood and falling over the side.

Bending, she blindly felt for it with her free hand, holding the pinafore with the other. The ferns about the pole announced her activity with rustling, but she was determined to gather every morsel.

Sensing something was amiss, she looked up. Her heart skipped and eyes widened. A dark figure stood at the rear corner of the house. It was the old man, the crossbow in his hands aimed directly at her.

Gripping her pinafore with both hands, she turned and sprinted towards the trees.

'Hey!'

She tensed at the sound of the man's voice, but didn't look back. Expectant of a bolt and intent on the blackness beneath the pines, she forced her weak body to run on.

Entering the trees, Oona began to weave between them in the hope they would protect her from the anticipated shot. The rush of blood filled her ears and she could not tell if the man was following, the thought that he was pursuing her driving Oona forward.

Exhaustion soon took its toll. Her steps became laboured and she slowed her pace for fear of losing her balance as she continued to grip the makeshift pouch. She risked a backward glance and saw nothing but the night.

Coming to a halt, her shoulders sagged and her face was chilled by cooling perspiration. An owl hooted and the trees whispered their secrets, but there was no evidence that the man was following her.

Oona listened for running water, absently dipping a hand into the pinafore and taking out a piece of flatbread. Putting it into her mouth and chewing slowly, she thought she discerned the sounds of the stream woven into those of the branches. Fighting her body's need for rest, she set off, longing for the shelter of the hollow.

4

'What was it Walt, another bear on the prowl after waking?' Dorothy sat in one of two armchairs before the fire, a patchwork shawl of pinks and reds about her thin shoulders.

He shook his head as he shut the door and leant the crossbow beside it, the quiver of bolts already resting there. 'A negro, would you believe?' he replied, slipping his boots off.

'A negro? In these parts?' She looked at him in surprise.

'Not just any negro,' he said, straightening and walking over. 'She were only a young-un.' He bent and kissed her forehead before stepping to the fire and examining the contents of the pot hanging above the flames. 'Coming on nicely,' he commented when he saw the stew stirred by heat, pieces of squirrel meat churning amidst the chopped vegetables.

'It was a girl?'

Walt nodded and took the second seat, reclining with a sigh of satisfaction. 'She was stealing from the tables.' He stretched his legs out, crossing his feet in front of the fire. 'I'd guess she's on the run and half starved.'

Dorothy glanced at the cooking pot, the smell of the stew thick in the single roomed cottage. 'There'd have been enough to go round.'

'There wasn't a chance to invite her. She was off into the night like a shot.'

She looked towards the door, gaze briefly settling on the crossbow. 'I ain't surprised,' she replied. 'I'd have run if I'd have seen a grizzled old fool carrying that thing.'

'This old fool got us the meat for our supper.'

'And has to use the sill to steady his aim now that his hands are too shaky.'

'It works, don't it?' he responded, raising a bushy white eyebrow.

'Of a fashion. What if you wanted to shoot a squirrel out back? There ain't no windows for you to be using.'

'Well, that makes for them being more comfortable coming around the front,' he grinned, front teeth missing and others rotting. 'I'm not just a pretty face.' He winked at his wife.

She shook her head and chuckled. 'You really are a daft old bird.'

'And you're the woman this daft old bird loves,' he responded.

'Honey tongue,' she joked as the fire crackled.

Dorothy got to her feet and looked in the pot. 'I'll dish up,' she stated, moving between the chairs and rubbing his wild hair affectionately as she went by.

She moved to a table at the back of the room and pulled out the left of two drawers beneath, taking out a ladle, along with a couple of spoons. Leaning against the edge of the table with her stomach, she reached for the pile of wooden bowls on the lowest shelf on the wall above.

Taking a pair down, she returned to the hearth and placed them on the piece of stone that rested before the fire. One of the logs spat an ember towards her and she looked down to check that her green woollen dress hadn't been burnt. Seeing that no harm had been done, she took up the ladle and the first of the bowls.

The serving done and spoons placed in the stew, she straightened and turned. Handing one to her husband, Dorothy returned to her seat, setting the bowl upon her lap and savouring the aroma as she pulled the shawl tight about her shoulders.

'For what we are about to receive,' said Dorothy, briefly bowing and closing her eyes, Walter already holding his spoon in readiness.

'Amen,' he said, closing their truncated grace and dipping the spoon in, beginning to eat despite the heat of the food. 'Mmm, tastes good.'

'I'll take your word for it for the time being,' she replied, lifting her bowl and blowing away the steam.

'It's no wonder I married you,' he smiled. 'You're the best cook in this territory, without a doubt.'

'Only in this territory?' She looked at him with eyebrow raised, the couple having adopted similar expressions in the years of their union.

'In the whole state and beyond,' he qualified, taking up another spoonful, a dribble running into his beard as he put it in his mouth.

Dorothy took a little of the stew onto her spoon, blowing again as she held it before her lips. Tentatively eating it, she nodded to herself. 'I dare say, you're right,' she said, smiling warmly at her husband, his blue eyes still filled with the same light that attracted her to him when only a young woman.

The snap and spit of the fire punctuated the sounds of their consumption as they ate in silence. Scraping his bowl and tipping the last into his mouth, Walt finished first and put his bowl on the floor beside his chair.

Rising, he placed a few more logs on the flames. 'You want some more?' he asked over his shoulder.

'I ain't halfway through as yet, but you help yourself.'

He reached back for his bowl and ladled more stew into it. Settling upon his chair, he began digging in immediately.

'Walter Stanley Brightwater!' she exclaimed with a shake of her head and chuckle, seeing the food almost spilling over the edge of his bowl after he'd filled it to the brim. 'You always did have an appetite big enough for the both of us.'

'It's just what a growing man needs,' he responded, his smile deepening the warm creases about his eyes.

'What about a shrinking man? I swear you used to be six foot when first we met.'

Walt laughed. 'Only when climbing a ladder.'

'Well, we did spend a lot of time in Pa's hayloft.' Her expression softened as she regarded her husband and recalled their recklessness.

'What is it?' he asked.

'Just remembering the farmhand who stole my heart.'

Walt's cheeks reddened. 'Not before you stole mine.'

Dorothy held her hand out towards him. He reached for it and they looked at each other adoringly for a few moments.

'Maybe I should go look for her,' said Walt as he began eating once again.

'The negro?'

He nodded, mouth full of stew.

'You ain't the best tracker in daylight, so you'd have no hope now. Go check for tracks in the morning, if you want, but I'll wager she's hightailed it of here by now. If she's a runaway, she's not going to want to stick around. She's likely heading north.'

'There's a lot of country for her to cover if she's going up there,' responded Walt as he continued to eat.

'She won't be the first to try.'

'Still, maybe I should go have a look around when morning comes.'

'When morning comes,' nodded Dorothy, gathering the last of her stew on her spoon and finishing her meal.

5

Oona woke to the wash of the stream's passage. Her lids lifted, remaining hooded as she stirred to the new day. The sun had risen, the day once again clear and the spring warmth already growing.

She brushed at irritation upon her cheek, an ant falling to the earth. She watched it circle, as if looking for the culprit. Leaning on her elbow, she raised herself up and rested against the back of the hollow.

Feeling the slight bulge of the pinafore, she was reminded of the food found during the night. She opened the makeshift pouch and peered at what remained. There were a couple of pieces of flatbread amidst a collection of nuts. She picked them out and ate them, finding her mouth dry.

She studied the nuts, only recognising pecans. Taking one, she put it between her teeth and forced the shell apart with the pressure of her bite. Spitting the pieces onto her palm, she picked out the kernel and discarded the rest. Selecting the other pecans, she tipped the other varieties of nut onto the ground and consumed the half dozen upon her hand.

Making her way out, the roof of the hollow brushing against her head, she went to the edge of the stream and drank, grateful for the fresh water to wash down the dry offerings. Staying crouched, she considered her next course of action.

'Stay longer or head north?' she asked, her words faintly echoing along the gully.

She shook her head, unable to come to a decision.

Her gaze was drawn by a flash in the water. A fish darted from one stone to another, finding concealment in the shadows beside.

'Be that a sign to stay?'

She nudged the second stone. The fish broke from cover and swam into the shallows at the edge of the stream. Its dorsal fin disturbed the surface in brief panic before it changed direction and returned to the current, vanishing downstream towards the creek.

'Or to go?' she said with a frown.

Deciding to clean herself, she made her way along the bank of mud. It gave way to stones and she began to balance her way towards the creek. Arms out to the sides, she treated the journey as a game, jumping from one rock to the next. The weight of her past was lost to the moment. The child that was so often crushed beneath was allowed its expression as she pirouetted and bounded. Beams of sunlight illuminated her dainty form as she giggled, experiencing a lightness of being such as she'd rarely felt.

Reaching the end of the gully, she moved out onto the rocks at the edge of the creek. Nearing the rushing waters, her right foot slipped.

She inhaled sharply as her ankle twisted and she fell forward. Her knee clashed with another stone, the impact jarring as she put her hands out to cushion the fall.

Oona turned over and sat between the rocks, the previous gaiety forgotten. She looked first to her knee, lifting the hem of her dress. There was redness, but no other trace of injury.

Turning her attention to her ankle, she could see swelling already beginning to show. Pushing up on a boulder, she found the joint unable to withstand use and nearly toppled for a second time as she let out a cry of pain.

She looked both ways along the creek, feeling exposed and worried that her presence would be detected. Almost on all fours, she made her way back towards the bank, the gully holding the promise of concealment.

'Hey there!'

She froze, cowering amidst the rocks.

'I ain't going to hurt you.'

She looked up to find the old man from the previous night standing not ten yards away, flanked by pines and wearing a fur hat with a squirrel tail hanging at the back. There was no sign of the crossbow. Instead, he carried a cloth-wrapped package under his arm.

Walt took it from where it was stowed and held it out to her. 'It's food, for you,' he offered.

She stared at him with unguarded suspicion. 'Why?'

'You look hungry and last night you were stealing scraps left for the birds and squirrels.' He stepped from the woodland and onto the first of the rocks bordering the creek. 'Here. Take it.'

Oona backed away, feeling anxious and aware that she was trapped between the man and the fast-flowing waters. 'What you want from me?' she asked.

Walt looked at her in puzzlement. 'We don't want nothing, other than for you to be well fed,' he answered with a forced smile, trying to gain her confidence.

'And you don't be wanting any kind of payment?'

'We've enough to share.'

Oona remained in station, her dark eyes filled with distrust.

'I tell you what. I'll leave it here and you can help yourself once I'm on my way,' he stated, placing the package on the rock in front of him. 'How's that sound?'

She made no reply.

He regarded her a moment, noting her sunken cheeks and the weary look of her eyes. Turning, he made his way into the pines.

'If you want that ankle seen to, Dotty can tend to it,' he said, pausing at the edge of the forest.

She continued to hold her tongue, watching as he turned and made his way back to the cottage.

6

Walt walked over to one of the bird tables as he approached the cottage. Checking that there were still a few scraps upon it, he then straightened the pole beneath. Looking at the trees about the clearing, he stood and savoured the birdsong for a while, gladdened by the spring return of so many species.

He walked to the house, stepping onto the porch and opening the door.

Dorothy stood before him with broom in hand, switches to the boards as she stopped and looked up. 'Either you found her or you ate the food yourself. The latter wouldn't surprise me at all.'

Walt smiled, leaving the door open on the new day and stepping over to her. Resting his hands on her hips, he gave her a kiss, the broom between them. 'Good to see you too,' he said, eyes sparkling as the first rays of sunshine penetrated the interior, motes of dust disturbed by Dorothy's cleaning catching in the golden light.

'Where was she?' she asked.

'At the creek. Looks like she's hurt herself.'

She looked into his eyes questioningly. 'Hurt herself?'

'Twisted her ankle on the rocks, by the looks of it.'

'She won't travel far like that,' responded Dorothy, glancing over his shoulder and out of the door.

'The food will help.'

She turned to him again. 'I wasn't sure she'd take it.'

'She didn't.'

Her brow creased and her expression conveyed a silent question.

'She wouldn't come near me, so I had to leave it on the bank. Her curiosity and hunger will see that she opens it.'

She considered and nodded.

Walt leant forward and kissed her again, hands sliding round to her backside and pulling her closer, the handle of the broom pressing against his chest. Dorothy noted the look in his eyes, a shiver of pleasure running through her.

'I ain't got time for that,' she stated despite her arousal, pushing him back with the broom.

'We've got all the time in the world,' he responded, gently taking the implement from her hands and meeting with little resistance.

She smiled coyly, lowering her gaze as he reached out and leant the broom against the table. Taking her into his arms, she raised her face to his and they kissed tenderly.

'Maybe we've a little time,' she conceded.

7

Oona sat on a large rock with the pines at her back and creek rushing by before her. She chewed on the last of the bread and cheese. The light upon the ripples danced within her dark eyes and played across her face. The food was settling, stomach groaning with thanks.

She looked at the remaining slivers of meat, the cloth lying open beside her. 'Not all white folk be the same,' she stated, repeating what Etty had told her on a number of occasions.

Looking over her shoulder, she thought about the man's offer concerning his wife tending her ankle. She turned her gaze to the inflamed injury. She couldn't head north until it was healed enough to take her weight. The choice she'd struggled to make had been made for her by circumstance. She had to stay, but fate had granted her another option beyond that of hunkering in the hollow.

She closed her eyes and felt the sun upon her cheeks. She saw Etty's face, the old slave's eyes filled with the wisdom she'd often bestowed. 'I wish you was here beside me,' she whispered.

Opening her eyes, Oona turned her attention to the scars, cuts and fading bruises about her wrists. The manacles had left a mark that would remain all her life, both physically and mentally.

She pulled down the sleeves of her dress in order to cover the evidence of ownership. Looking south along the creek, she wondered if the farmhands still sought her whereabouts. She pictured the hounds sniffing at undergrowth and earth, seeking out her scent. Handlers kept hold of the leashes while riders waited for a fresh trail, rifles holstered at their saddles.

Her tension evident in the tightness of her shoulders, Oona shook her head and tried to rid herself of the unhelpful images. She took up one of the slivers from the cloth and chewed off the end, mouth salivating in response to the preserving salt rubbed into the flesh. The taste was unfamiliar, though it bore a similarity to rat, which had supplemented her meagre diet many times at the plantation.

'It may be squirrel,' she mumbled, tearing off another piece.

She thought about the old man who'd brought the food. Recalling his expression when she'd discovered him standing by the cottage, she could discern no hint of malice. There certainly had been none that morning by the creek, and she started to seriously consider the offer of treatment.

Gently pushing her sole against one of the rocks in front of her, she winced and quickly released the pressure. Tears of pain had arisen and she wiped them away with the back of her hand, noting the branch trapped between rocks a little way downstream.

Taking the edge of the cloth, she covered the rest of the meat and placed a small stone atop in order to keep birds from the food. She awkwardly made her way towards the branch, her hands acting to support her more often than not.

Reaching her intended destination, she crawled out onto the first of the rocks, its surface warm to the touch after being bathed in sunlight. Resting on her stomach when she reached the far side, she stretched for the branch, which was just out of reach.

Oona moved up a little, her shoulders over the side. The extra reach meant that she was able to grasp the branch, the tangle of debris that hung from it slippery and damp to the touch thanks to the frothing of the stream a foot below.

She pulled. The branch bent and shifted, but did not come free.

Adjusting her grip, she drew the branch towards her to loosen the far end. With another tug, it came free and she backed away from the drop. Turning, she sat up and ripped away the debris, letting it tumble to the side.

She put the narrowest end to a rock. Pressing down on the other, which was knotted and askew from the main length, she tested its strength. It did not break and seemed sturdy enough to take her weight.

She grasped the knots, her fingers resting between and finding it a comfortable hold. 'A good handle,' she commented, pushing herself up.

Taking a few tentative steps as she got used to using the novel walking stick, she smiled and nodded. 'This will do,' she said, happy with her utilisation of the branch.

Oona looked to the pines, pondering the invitation once again. 'Not all white folk be the same,' she repeated to herself by way of reassurance.

Making her way to where the cloth rested, she took the stone from it and tied the corners. Holding it in her free hand, she traversed the rocks and went into the trees, grateful when the rough ground gave way to the needled earth.

'Not all white folk be the same,' she said once more, bolstering her courage as she made her way between the trunks.

8

Dorothy stood with broom in hand, wearing a deep blue dress and hair tied back as she brushed dirt from the porch. She lifted her head to movement in the periphery of her vision and set eyes on the black girl materialising out of the tree line to her left. Falling still, she watched the nervous approach, which reminded her of a wild animal wary of prey.

Oona glanced about the clearing. Her muscles were tensed despite the fact that her ankle hampered any chance of fleeing from potential danger. The middle-aged woman on the porch remained motionless. She could see no sign of the man, his absence increasing her agitation.

She came to a halt halfway from the pines.

'My name's Dotty,' offered the woman, forcing a smile.

Oona said nothing.

'What's your name?'

'Where be the man?'

'He's off panhandling,' replied Dorothy. 'He's trying to find gold in the creek,' she added when she saw the lack of comprehension in the girl's expression.

Oona looked back at the relative safety of the trees as she considered turning tail.

'Don't go,' pleaded Dorothy, leaning the broom against the wall and taking a step down from the porch. 'Did you like the food?'

She returned her attention to the woman.

'We helped see to your hunger and it may be we can help with your injury too.' She nodded towards the girl's feet, sympathy arising in response to her enfeebled condition. 'You could rest up here until you're healed.'

'You'd let me stay?' Oona eyed her suspiciously. If there was one thing she had come to know, it was that negroes didn't share the homes of whites.

'There ain't much room inside, but I'm sure we can fix up someplace for you to rest your head,' confirmed Dorothy.

Oona began to back away, sure that there was some ulterior motive at play. Despite Etty's words, she could not trust an offer that went so far beyond the bounds of her experience at the hands of white folk.

'Please.' Dotty took another step and extended a hand towards her. 'I only want to help.'

Oona continued to retreat towards the pines.

'Think of the food Walt left for you,' encouraged Dorothy. 'It was given without expectation, freely and with purely Christian motive.'

'Christian motive?'

'We helped without any wish for anything in return and without judgement.'

Oona glanced at the loosely tied package in her left hand, pondering what the woman had said.

Dorothy saw the indecision, noting that the girl's retreat had come to a stop. She began to walk towards her, a smile upon her face. 'At least let me take a look at your ankle and then you can be on your way, if that's what you wish.'

Oona made no movement, watching the approach with continued caution.

Slowing her pace as she neared, Dorothy drew up before the girl. 'I'll just take a look,' she stated, lowering onto her haunches. 'Do you mind if I touch it to find out the extent of the injury?'

She didn't reply.

Dotty reached forward, seeing the additional stiffness of the girl's posture. She placed her fingers to the skin and began to conduct her examination. Oona tensed on a couple of occasions, breath becoming sharp and indicating the areas of most pain.

'Well,' said Dorothy as she straightened, 'it ain't broken, but it is badly sprained.'

'What do that mean?'

'It means you shouldn't be putting any weight on it for a few days. The best thing you can do is rest up and keep it still. The healing will take place naturally.'

'I have the stick,' responded Oona.

'And we have food to help you mend. I can also make a tonic to ease the pain.'

'*If* I stay,' she said with emphasis on the first word.

Dorothy looked into her eyes. 'If you don't, I'll give you more food to take with you so you can keep up your strength.' She held her hand out towards the cloth.

Oona glanced down.

'I'll fill it with what we can spare,' explained Dotty. 'Then you can be on your way.'

She tentatively passed the cloth to the woman, quickly withdrawing her hand. Dotty turned and began to walk away, dress lightly stained by dust.

'Will you give me your name?' asked the woman without turning.

'Oona,' she replied distractedly, looking around the clearing. With a deep breath, she set off after the woman.

'How old are you?' asked Dorothy over her shoulder as she neared the cottage.

'Thirteen.'

'Really?' she responded with a backward glance. 'You're small for your age,' she added as she stepped onto the porch and disappeared from view.

Oona's gaze moved to the open window as she limped towards the front door. She saw no sign of Dorothy, finding only shadows within. The idea that the crossbow was being aimed at her by the woman's husband came to mind, bringing her to a halt a few steps shy of the cottage.

'You can come in if you want, Oona,' called Dotty.

Sidestepping to the right, she was afforded a view of the woman at the back of the room. Dorothy was crouching as she looked into a cabinet, hunting out foodstuffs to place upon the cloth that had been laid on the table beside her. There was no sign of her husband, though the edge of the crossbow could be seen leaning by the front door.

Emboldened by the sight of the weapon and the knowledge that Dotty was indeed searching out food, she made her way onto the porch. She moved to stand in the doorway, peering into the abode and viewing the simplicity of its interior. The faint smell of wood smoke filled her nostrils and she noted a bed resting in the far left corner. A small rug lay upon the floorboards beside, its colours foot-stained and faded.

Turning to the opposite end of the room, she saw two armchairs placed in front of the hearth, a patchwork shawl resting over the back of the nearest. Her gaze was drawn to shelves on the back wall beyond the chairs. Upon them was an assortment of carvings. Most were of birds, some with wings outstretched and others at rest. At the centre was a stag's head, antlers rising high.

'Who carved those?' She nodded toward the figures.

'Walter,' answered Dorothy as she straightened and stepped to the table, placing more bread on the cloth as she glanced over at the girl. 'I sew and he carves to pass the time on long winter nights. We could teach you how to do both, if you decide to stay.'

Oona looked at her as she placed a piece of cheese on the table and took a sheet of brown paper from the right-hand drawer beneath. Wrapping the offering, she tied the packet with brown cord.

'Would you like a little more squirrel meat to go with what you have left?'

'What you've done given me is enough.'

Dorothy retied the bundle and took it to the door, holding it out to the girl, whose diminutive shadow was cast into the house. 'Here.'

Oona took it and looked at the other woman, studying her expression closely. 'Be I truly free to leave?'

She nodded. 'If that's what you want,' she replied without a hint of deception.

Oona hesitated in the doorway. 'If I be staying with you, can I leave anytime I wish it?'

'Yes,' confirmed Dotty. 'You can stay as long as you want and choose to leave when you want.'

The girl stood in thought, glancing down at the food package in her hand. 'I will stay tonight,' she said eventually.

'I'm glad,' responded Dorothy with a genuine smile. 'We can make you up a place to sleep in the near corner there,' she said, pointing to the right of the chimney breast. 'I have a couple of blankets; one to act as a cover and the other to soften the harshness of the floorboards against your back.'

'You really be letting me stay indoors?'

Dorothy's smile lost its vigour as she grasped why the girl would make such an enquiry. 'We ain't like other folk you may have come across, Oona.'

'We slept in a bunkhouse at the plantation,' said the girl. 'It weren't more than a shack, and not a good one. There were many a time I be thinking the wind would bring it down on our heads,' she added, recalling it howling through holes in the slats on stormy nights, bringing to mind wolves and other fell beasts.

'Well, we ain't got a bunkhouse or even an outhouse for you to be sleeping in, so it's inside or out on the porch,' responded Dotty. 'One has a fire and good company, the other a serious draft problem.' She winked at the girl.

Oona couldn't help but smile. 'A fire sounds good,' she said, her previous apprehension quickly evaporating as the sun warmed her back.

'Then it's settled?'

'Yes,' nodded Oona.

9

They were bathed in sunlight as they sat on the edge of the porch and ate side by side. Instead of using the food she'd packaged for the girl, Dorothy had opted to take more from the cupboard, wanting Oona to feel secure in her ability to leave when she saw fit.

'How's the cheese?' she asked

'Good,' replied Oona with a nod, her walking stick leaning beside her.

'Ezra, our son, brings it from Atlanta. He's the spit of Walter and lives in Fulton County. He visits when he can.'

'You have other children?' asked Oona through a mouthful of bread and cheese.

Dorothy's expression dropped slightly. 'Just Ezra,' she stated with a touch of melancholy.

Oona studied her profile, detecting a deep sadness. 'How old be he?'

'Twenty-eight. He's married to a German immigrant called Johanna who's a few years younger.' Dotty turned to her. 'They have children of their own,' she said with a strained smile, her eyes still betraying darkness within.

'What be his work?'

Dorothy looked down at the food on her lap. 'He runs a cotton mill,' she said with decreased volume, feeling a pang of guilt that her son should work in a trade associated with slavery.

'You must be proud,' she replied sincerely.

Dotty turned to her, wondering at her origins. 'Where do you come from?'

Oona went still. 'From the west,' she said evasively, not turning to meet the woman's gaze.

Observing her body language and the sudden tightness of the girl's expression, Dorothy felt certain that they'd been correct in their estimation that she was a runaway. 'Well, it don't matter now,' she reassured. 'You're here with us and can stay as long as you see fit.'

Oona remained tense as she began eating once again, sidling away from Dotty when the woman's attention was focussed on the birds feeding at the tables.

'Walt never shoots the birds,' commented Dorothy, wishing to dispel the strained atmosphere that had settled between them, 'and he only kills what we need when it comes to the squirrels.'

'Like the Injuns,' mumbled Oona.

'Pardon?'

'Like the Injuns. They only take what they be needing. That's what Etty done told me.'

'True,' said Dotty with a nod. 'If we all take more than our needs dictate, then one day there'll be no world left to sustain us.'

'Sustain?' asked Oona, finally turning to the woman.

'Keep us going.'

'So, you decided to join us then?'

Both women turned to Walter's approach. His britches were darkened by dampness and he carried a wide pan, the sleeves of his shirt rolled up.

'Any luck?' asked Dotty.

He shook his head as he strolled over to them, glancing at a bird table as he passed. 'We need to top them up.'

'The birds have been hungry this morning,' responded his wife.

Walt drew to a halt a few yards in front of them, briefly scratching at his wild grey beard.

'Oona, this is Walter. Walter, this is Oona,' introduced Dorothy.

'Glad to make your acquaintance,' he stated with a smile.

'And yours,' she responded, her features filled with renewed tension.

'May I join you?'

'As long as you don't expect me to be getting up and fetching your food,' replied Dotty.

'I know you too well to expect anything of the sort,' he replied cheekily before moving to the side and stepping around his wife, careful not to encroach on the girl's space.

Oona listened intently to Walter's activity within the cottage, hearing his boots upon the boards and the pan being placed on the table.

'There ain't much cheese left,' he called.

'Ezra should be along sometime soon,' replied Dotty. 'He'll be bringing plenty more, I'm sure.'

'I hope he remembers my tobacco.'

'I hope he forgets,' whispered Dotty conspirationally, leaning towards Oona. 'Makes the place stink like you wouldn't believe.'

'I heard that,' said Walter as he took bread from the cupboard at the rear of the room.

'Good,' responded Dorothy. 'Maybe you'll take notice of your wife this time and stop smoking that old pipe of yours.'

Walter's footsteps announced his return. He walked behind Dotty and seated himself on the far side. 'You can see why I married her,' he said, leaning forward and speaking across his wife, winking at Oona before beginning to eat.

10

Oona sat cross-legged on the boards to the right of Dorothy's armchair. Her hand rested on her lap, empty bowl upon the palm. Her stomach groaned in appreciation of the food she'd consumed as flames danced in her gaze. She'd eaten with the haste of someone who wasn't certain of when the next meal may come, both Dorothy and Walter still spooning the watery casserole from their bowls as they sat on the chairs.

The former finished up, chasing a piece of meat around the side of her bowl before finally using her thumb to help slide it onto the spoon. 'I should make up your sleeping area,' she stated after swallowing.

The words didn't register; Oona transfixed by the fire.

'Oona.' Dorothy reached out and touched the girl's shoulder.

She was given a start and turned to her in shock, reaching towards the stick that rested on the floorboards nearby as if preparing to make an escape.

'Sorry, I didn't mean to give you a fright,' she apologised. 'I was just saying that I ought to see to your sleeping arrangements.'

Oona nodded, breathing deeply to reduce the beating of her heart and hand returning to her lap.

'Let me take that.' Dorothy leant forward and held out her hand, nodding towards the bowl.

She handed it over.

'Seconds, me thinks,' said Walter, rising from his seat and stepping to the pot over the fire.

Dorothy got up and walked between the armchairs, Oona keeping a careful eye on both of them, not yet fully convinced of their good intentions. She'd been offered Dotty's seat, but had chosen to sit on the floor so that she was closest to the door should she need to make an exit.

Dorothy went to the bed in the far corner as Walter ladled more food into his bowl. Kneeling on the rug, she grasped the handle of a small chest stowed beneath, her husband looking over while going back to his chair. With the scrape of wood on wood, she pulled it out and undid the single catch. Mustiness touched with mould lifted into the air as she opened the slightly curved top, resting it against the edge of the bed. Rummaging inside, she pulled out two folded grey blankets and placed them on her knees.

After another brief search, she closed the lid and refastened the chest before pushing it back under the bed. Sidling closer to the head of the cot, she reached for an open-topped wooden box which was twice the size of the chest, taking hold of the sides and drawing it out.

Dorothy rifled through the clothes and pieces of material contained inside. Discovering a roll of rough brown woollen cloth at the bottom, she slipped it out and unravelled it. 'Just enough to make a pillow,' she stated, looking over her shoulder at Oona as she held it up.

Pushing the box into its storage space, the effort causing her to slide back a little, she took hold of the blankets and length of cloth before getting to her feet. Walking to the table, she took a leather case from the furthest of the drawers before returning to her seat and settling herself.

'There's still some left,' said Walter. 'Is anyone going to mind if I have thirds?'

Dorothy looked down at Oona with raised eyebrows and shook her head. 'He ain't got a stomach, he's got a bottomless pit,' she commented as Walt got up and went to ladle out the last of supper.

'With your cooking, there's no wonder I want more,' he responded.

Dotty chuckled. 'Charmer,' she said with a loving glance.

'What be in the case?' enquired Oona, looking at the rectangular box resting atop the cloth and blankets upon Dorothy's lap.

'This,' she replied, taking hold of the hardened leather case in readiness to open it, 'is my sewing kit.'

She flipped the lid up as Walter retook his seat. A selection of needles were secured in black cloth on the underside. Spindles of cotton occupied the deeper bottom half, a few stray buttons scattered beneath and a small pair of scissors amidst them.

'If I make a start now, it may be I can have it done before bedtime,' she stated. 'And it may be you can have a try, if you fancy it.'

'I'll watch,' responded Oona.

Dorothy slipped one of the needles from the case and selected a roll of brown cotton. 'This should do nicely,' she said as Walter raised his bowl and tipped the last of his third helping into his mouth.

'Beg your pardon,' he said after burping loudly.

'Well, I never,' declared Dotty. 'That's the first time he's apologised for breaking any kind of wind since we moved from the city, nigh on fifteen year ago.'

Oona smiled.

'There ain't no need when it's just the two of us,' said Walter.

'That's what you think,' she replied, turning to the girl. 'Sometimes I'm in want of a peg for my nose.' Dorothy waved a hand before her face, her expression one of mock disgust.

A brief laugh escaped Oona's lips, amused by the couples' banter and feeling increasingly at ease.

'Why don't you sit yourself up here?' Dotty patted the arm of the chair.

Scratching her head in thought for a moment as she came to a decision, Oona awkwardly got to her feet, trying to put minimal weight on her ankle. She sat on the edge of the arm, good foot to the floor to keep her balance. Snapping the sewing kit shut and placing it on the other side from the girl, Dorothy leant forward and laid the blankets by her feet.

'Now,' she said, laying the brown cloth upon her lap, 'this looks to be about perfect. It seems that the Good Lord was expecting you.'

'Expecting me?' asked Oona.

'I don't think it's a coincidence that there's just enough to make you a pillow. I think you were meant to stay with us.' She smiled warmly up at her.

'Really?'

'Of course,' she replied with a nod. 'I feel The Lord's guiding hand at work,' she added, certain that the girl had not been brought to them by hap of chance.

Oona thought about what she'd said as Dorothy threaded the needle and arranged the cloth in readiness to begin sewing. She'd never come across white folk that treated negroes in such a way and the idea that God had caused her to come across them was a comforting one. Despite having committed a great sin, He was still watching over her. There was still hope for her soul.

'Maybe I ain't damned,' she whispered as she stared at the fire.

'What was that?' asked Dorothy, looking up with the needle held at the ready.

Oona blinked and turned to the woman. 'Nothing,' she replied, a blush upon her cheeks and unable to hold her gaze.

Dotty studied her expression, deciding not to make further enquiry. Returning her attention to the cloth upon her lap, she made a start and began to sew one of the sides of the pillow. 'Let me know if you want to take a turn,' she said without looking at the girl. 'We'll stuff it with some rags once there's only one end left to stitch.'

Oona watched the needle weave in and out of the brown cloth. Dorothy worked with practiced ease as Walter arose from his seat and went to the shelves in the corner where the carvings rested. Taking a partially completed bird from the lowest, he took up a small knife and whetstone.

Returning to his seat, he blew Dorothy a kiss when she glanced over. She smiled, blowing one back before focussing on the sewing once again. Checking the sharpness of the blade and finding it fit for purpose, Walt placed the stone on the far arm and began to whittle at the bird's open wings. Bending close, he narrowed his eyes as he began to add detailed feathering, his tongue poking out as he carefully drew the point along the wood.

Oona observed him for a time, shavings falling to his knees and often tumbling to the floorboards. The couple concentrated on their tasks with an air of contentment. They were wordless, without affectation or self-consciousness.

'Honest,' she muttered, the word summing up their unguarded appearance.

'Pardon?' asked Dotty without looking up.

'I'll stitch the last end,' she said, thinking quickly.

'I'll fetch out the rags to use as stuffing while you do,' said Dorothy.

'I can get them,' responded Oona.

Dotty glanced at the girl's swollen ankle. 'You sure?'

Oona nodded, slipping from the arm and reaching down for her walking stick. 'I want to be of help.'

'They're in the sack under the foot of the bed.'

'Could you put a couple more logs on the fire, while you're at it?' added Walter.

She hobbled to the woodpile left of the chimney and did as asked before making her way over to the cot, stick tapping on the boards. Taking out the sack, she opened it and looked at the tatty clothing and rags inside, wondering how much to take over.

'Just bring the sack,' said Dorothy over her shoulder, as if reading her mind.

Oona made her way back and placed the sack by the woman's feet.

'Do you want to stuff it?' she enquired, all but one end of the case neatly stitched and the needle tucked into the cloth at the corner in readiness to sew it up.

'How much should I be putting in?' she replied, bending as Dorothy opened the pillowcase towards her.

'Enough that you'll be comfortable.'

Oona took out a handful of rags and pushed them in, Dotty keeping a firm hold.

'One more should do. What do you think?'

She nodded and took out more. Placing them into the case, she found that it was only half full.

'Don't fret, when they're spread evenly throughout, it'll be a comfortable rest for your head,' smiled Dorothy, noting the girl's dissatisfied expression.

She turned it on her lap so that the opening was facing her and rearranged the rags within. 'There,' she stated, holding it up, 'that's better. Now all that's left is for you to sew up the end. Do you want to sit here?'

'I'll sit on the floor,' replied Oona.

'As you will,' said Dotty.

She settled on the boards by the armchair and crossed her legs, setting the stick beside her.

Leaning over the arm, Dorothy passed her the pillow, glancing at the scars about the girl's wrists. 'Mind you don't prick yourself.'

Oona slipped the needle from its resting place and looked at Dotty's stitching in order to gauge the distance between each pass through the cloth. Pushing the point through, she started sealing the pillow, glancing up at the woman to check she was doing so correctly.

Dorothy nodded and smiled encouragingly. Feeling more confident with each stitch, Oona soon finished, pulling the needle through one final time.

'You want me to secure it?'

She gave a nod and handed the pillow to the woman, who picked up the small scissors resting in the sewing kit and snipped the thread. Securing it, she examined the girl's work. 'Not bad at all.'

Oona peered over the arm. Her stitching was undoubtedly rougher than Dorothy's and not as straight, but there were no sizeable gaps or loose passes.

'You can sleep with a little more comfort now,' said Dotty, handing the pillow over to her. 'I'll set the blankets down for you.'

She picked up the blankets and got out of her seat. Going to the right of the chimneybreast, she unfolded the first and placed it on the floor. 'Are you wanting to be sleeping with your head or feet to the fire?' she asked.

'Head.'

Laying the second blanket on top of the first, she folded back the near end. 'It ain't much, but it'll serve.'

'Much obliged,' responded Oona.

Dorothy straightened and looked over to her husband as he continued to carve. 'You ready for bed yet?' she said after yawning.

Walter took no notice, his concentration fixed on the bird.

'Walt!'

He turned to her sharply, a look of confusion upon his face. 'You speaking to me?'

'I was trying to, but carving always seems to make you deaf,' she replied. 'I think it's about time we were to our bed.'

He nodded, scratching at his beard and glancing at the bird, the detail on one of its outstretched wings almost finished. 'Maybe just a little longer.'

'We've a guest that could probably do with some rest,' she said pointedly.

Walter glanced at Oona before turning his gaze back to his wife. 'Right you are,' he said, brushing shavings from his knees before rising.

Oona looked at the bucket tucked in the shadows beyond the front door.

'I think we should take the bucket out to the side of the house,' said Dorothy, catching the girl's look as Walter went to the shelving and put the carving, whetstone and knife back in place.

He turned to her questioningly and she glanced at Oona. Without needing to voice his query, he gave a shallow nod and walked over to the vessel that was used for their relief. Taking it by the handle, he took the tin pail out of the cottage.

'There, that'll allow for a little privacy,' said Dorothy, turning to Oona.

A thought struck her. 'I should fetch out one of Walt's old shirts to serve as a nightgown,' she stated, immediately making for the bed and crouching beside it.

Pulling out the box, she took out an old grey shirt and held it up. 'What do you think?'

Oona nodded. 'My thanks.'

Dorothy slid the box back as Walter re-entered the cottage.

'Thought I'd go while I was out there,' he said to explain his slight delay in returning.

'You can go next,' said Dotty as she walked over and handed Oona the shirt, 'though you may want to be changing in front of the fire. It still gets nippy out there after nightfall.'

The girl took the shirt and draped it over her arm, walking stick in hand. She went to the door and stepped out onto the porch with a backward glance. The interior was lit by a warm glow as Walter moved towards the cot, unbuttoning his shirt as he went. Dorothy had stepped to her armchair in order to retrieve her sewing kit.

Oona frowned as she closed the door, an ache in her heart. Despite her initial misgivings, she already felt at home. The warmth of the fire was outdone by the warmth of the couple who had taken her in, but this brought her lack of blood family into sharp relief.

'I be alone,' she whispered sadly as she looked either way along the porch and saw the edge of the bucket at the right corner of the cottage.

Once finished, she went back inside wearing the shirt, its hem halfway down her thighs and clothes tucked beneath her arm.

Dorothy turned from the table at the back of the room and smiled at her, noting that the sleeves were a good few inches too long. 'If you decide to stay for a while, I'll have to take the arms up for you.'

Oona glanced at her hands, which were hidden by the cotton. Raising the left she waved it in the air, the excess material flopping back and forth. 'At least it be keeping my hands warm.'

'True,' nodded Dorothy as she made her way over, giving the girl's head an affectionate rub as she passed and went out of the door.

Oona looked over at Walter, who was sitting on the edge of the bed in a long nightshirt. 'Night,' she stated, stepping over to where the blankets and pillow rested by the chimneybreast.

'Goodnight, Oona,' he replied. 'Sleep well.'

She settled herself facing the room, laying the stick on the floor beside the blankets. Despite the comfort she felt in their company, she could not bring herself to turn her back on the interior. After years of sleeping with the bunkhouse wall behind her so she could be alert to the master's night time visits, it was a habit she found hard to break.

Dorothy entered in a pale nightie, bare feet padding on the floor as she walked over to the bed. Walter got to his feet as she approached and they knelt side by side after she'd placed her clothes over a small dresser by the foot of the cot.

With their backs to the room, they placed their hands together, closing their eyes and bowing their heads.

'Dear Lord,' began Dorothy. 'We thank You for another blessed day in this paradise of Your making. We thank You also for bringing Oona to us, may she find refuge with us for as long as You see fit. May You grant us the wisdom and kindness to be good Christians and watch over us during the hours of darkness.'

'Amen,' they said together.

Oona watched at they kissed and climbed into bed, Walter moving over to the far side. She was gladdened by the mention of her name in the brief prayer and her eyes glistened.

'Thank you, Lord,' she whispered, closing her eyes and finding that sleep came easily.

11

She swung to and fro in the pitch black. There was only darkness and motion. The manacles about her wrists had been hung over one of the meat hooks that dangled from the low roof of the shed. They dug into her flesh and her shoulders ached. She could smell the beef carcasses hanging in the darkness with her and feel their crowded closeness.

Oona wriggled and struggled against her suspended captivity, but to no avail. She tried to call for help, finding her voice stolen by the tightness of her throat.

The door to the meat locker opened and a figure was silhouetted by faint moonlight. It was her master, his tall and lean physique unmistakable after so many visitations and punishments. In his hand was a riding crop. In his demeanour was intent.

He stepped into the locker, boots thudding ominously on the boards.

She screamed.

Oona woke as she lay on her back, eyes snapping open. Temporarily confused by her location, she looked about in the gloom. The grey light of dawn seeped between the shutters of the window and afforded her a little illumination. She could hear snoring across the room and recent memories came to the fore, her disorientation quickly passing.

She took a breath to calm her racing heart. Yawning, she found the figure of her master waiting for her behind her closed lids.

She shuddered as she opened her eyes once again, the dream refusing to dissipate into the chill morning.

Rubbing at her wrists, an ache apparent within their bones, she sat up.

Quietly getting onto all fours, Oona collected the covering blanket about her shoulders. She moved in front of the hearth and settled on her knees. With a glance towards the cot hidden in the shadows on the far side of the room, she took up the poker leaning beside and prodded at the ashes in the grate. Embers were revealed and she could feel their faint warmth against her hands.

Looking to the log pile, she reached for a couple of small pieces of wood and carefully placed them into the fireplace. Leaning forward, she blew on the embers visible between, their glow increasing.

After sustained encouragement, the first flames took to the logs and she rested back. Holding her hands out to the growing heat, she found her thoughts drifting. She surprised herself by imagining a life at the cottage, tending to the bird tables and contented with the simple existence.

Oona shook her head, trying to dismiss the idea, but finding it persistent. 'It hasn't yet been a day,' she scolded in a whisper. 'My imagination be running away with me again, Etty,' she added, picturing the motherly old slave.

Looking over her shoulder as the snoring continued, her musings turned to the couple with whom she found herself. They were different from any white folk she'd previously met. Any doubt about their earnestness had been ushered away by their kind words and deeds. She could detect no falsehood, no malice, only a Christian nature of kindness and sharing.

'It may be I can stay here for a good length of time,' she said, turning her attention back to the fire, the flames growing more vigorous and their flicker lighting her youthful features.

The bed creaked and the snoring stopped. Its occupants stirred and she heard Dotty yawn, letting out a groan as she did so. There was more movement and Oona glanced over. Dorothy was sitting and rubbing her eyes, brown hair messed by sleep.

Seeing the girl before the fire, she got to her feet. Gathering a patchwork of squirrel furs that rested atop the bed cover and placing it about her shoulders like a cloak, she walked over, sockets darkened by tiredness.

'Everything all right?'

Oona nodded. 'I hope you don't be minding me stoking the fire.'

'It's a pleasure to rise and find it alight,' replied Dorothy, moving to stand beside the girl. 'Did you sleep well?' she enquired, crouching and shuddering as a shiver passed through her.

Oona's expression dropped slightly and she turned to the fire in order to try and hide the change. 'Yes, thank you.'

'Good. I'm glad Walt's snoring didn't disturb you,' smiled Dotty.

Oona glanced at her, the only snoring she'd heard having arisen from the woman.

'The pillow we made clearly did the trick,' she said with a glance towards it.

The girl nodded. 'Better than any I've had before.'

'At the plantation?'

Oona gave another nod of response.

Dorothy studied her profile. 'Did you run away?'

Her cheeks reddened as she stared at the fire, not knowing if she should answer with the truth.

'It don't matter if you did. Me and Walt ran away too.'

Oona turned to her. 'You were slaves?' she said doubtfully.

'No,' replied Dorothy with a shake of her head. 'We ran away from the city to find a simpler life.'

'Would you mind keeping your voices down? Some of us are still trying to get some sleep.'

Oona and Dotty looked over to the cot, able to make out the presence of Walter beneath the covers as the light steadily grew and the fire helped to brighten the interior.

'He's always a little grouchy in the mornings,' she whispered. 'Some of us should be getting up and seeing to their chores,' she said aloud.

'There ain't nothing pressing to be seen to.'

'No? Them shingles on the porch roof ain't going to appear of their own accord.'

'I told you, I'll be about it when spring comes.'

'Well, it's come and you ain't been about it. I know you're getting on, but your joints ain't seized up yet,' she said with a sideways glance at the girl, a wide grin evident upon her face.

Oona stifled a chuckle.

'They don't complain as much as you either,' retorted Walter, the tone of his voice one of amusement. 'My sweetness,' he added.

Dorothy laughed. 'I'll get the oatmeal cooking if you'll rouse those old bones.'

He slowly sat up on the far side of the bed. 'A morning kiss would help.'

'Would it now?' She stood and walked over to the other side of the room. Leaning across the bed, she gave him a kiss and ruffled his thinning hair. 'Good morning, handsome.'

'Morning, gorgeous,' he responded, grinning at her and cupping her cheek in his palm. 'Nothing beats waking to you.' His free hand moved towards her chest, the nightie hanging open slightly and her cleavage visible.

'We have a guest,' she reminded him quietly, taking hold of his wrist and halting the advance.

'Sorry, I was a little distracted,' he replied.

'By what?'

He glanced down her top, raising his eyebrows as he looked back up at her.

She shook her head and frowned as she straightened. 'Trust you.'

'I was also distracted by the sight of the most beautiful woman in the world.'

She snorted. 'I think someone's eyesight must be failing. Now, get yourself up and I'll see to breakfast.'

'Maybe later,' he said quietly as she began to move towards the table, Dorothy glancing back to find him winking at her.

12

Oona sat beside Dorothy on the edge of the porch, both still wearing their night clothes. The morning sun rested upon their faces and empty bowls upon their laps, dregs of porridge about the edges yellowed by the honey that Dotty had added to sweeten the meal.

'This is my habit when the weather is fine,' commented the woman, leaning back with palms to the boards and closing her eyes to savour the warmth. 'When we lived in Atlanta, there weren't no sun to be had apart from late in the afternoon, such were the shadows of the buildings around us.'

'We ate what breakfast we had at benches alongside the bunkhouse,' responded Oona, waving away a large fly that took interest in her bowl.

Dorothy opened her eyes and squinted as she looked at the back of the girl's head. Her gaze moved to Oona's left hand, coming to rest on the scars and healing cuts about her wrist. 'What drove you to run?'

Oona scratched the side of her head as she thought on her reply. 'Cruelty,' she replied.

Dotty waited for her to expand, but no further explanation was forthcoming. 'Well, there'll be only kindness here,' she said with a smile.

The girl didn't turn, but stared at a couple of small brown birds squabbling over the food on the table furthest from the cottage.

'How's the ankle?'

'It throbs,' replied Oona, looking down at the swollen joint.

'Once we're dressed, we'll go foraging. There's some roots and leaves that will sooth the injury. How does that sound?'

The girl nodded. 'Much obliged.'

They fell into silence. Dorothy studied Oona's profile, seeing the downcast expression upon her face. She wanted to comfort her, to place an arm about her shoulders, but fought the urge, worried that the unexpected contact would discomfort the girl.

The shadow of the plantation darkened Oona's mind, brought forth by Dotty's enquiry. The sensations of helplessness and fear that her nightmare had evoked came back to her and she felt her body tense in response.

She put her bowl aside and gathered her knees to her chest. She held them close, hands clasping her arms, the sleeves of Walter's old shirt rolled up to her elbows. Gooseflesh hinted at the chill she felt within, skin tingling and hairs on end. The air about her felt as though it were thicker, pressing in and unable to sustain her lungs.

Oona breathed deeply, feeling her chest expanding against her legs, but finding no benefit. She saw the razor in her hand and spurts of blood falling to the boards.

The touch of Dorothy's hand upon her shoulder made her jump.

'You all right?'

Oona snatched up her stick and stood up. 'I need to be stretching my legs,' she stated, taking a few steps from the porch and unable to meet the woman's gaze as the sudden race of her heart began to calm.

'Don't you want to be getting changed first?' Dorothy looked up at her with concern, shading her eyes with a hand.

She shook her head. 'I won't be long.'

Oona hobbled away, heading south. She needed solitude, which had been rarely found on the plantation.

As she walked into the trees, she took in the scent of the pines and songs of the birds. They ushered the shadow of her past into the recesses of her mind, bringing a growing peace.

Glancing back, she saw that the cottage was hidden from sight. Her tension lifted further and she followed the sound of a small stream, soon arriving at its mossy bank.

Seeing a suitable rock, she made her way upstream. 'Must empty into the creek,' she mumbled to herself as the end of the walking stick left indentations in the soft soil and moss.

Seating herself and leaning the stick beside, Oona closed her eyes and let the soft burbling wash through her, cleansing the last of the darkness from her mind. Beams of sunlight were reflected by the ripples and danced upon her eyelids as she found restfulness.

The brush of material against bark caught Oona's attention. Her eyes snapped open, pulse quickening as she stared across the stream. Five yards into the trees on the far side stood two Indian girls. One was about her age and held the hand of the younger, who was no more than six. They appeared to be sisters and were dressed in skins, their black hair plaited and decorated with downy feathers.

'Naturals,' whispered Oona, using the term Etty had used to describe them.

Unsure what to do, she slowly raised her hand in greeting, feeling no threat from the pair. The youngest glanced up at her sister and then echoed the gesture.

Oona smiled softly, lowering her hand to scratch her nose.

The young native aped her movements, a grin upon her face.

Guessing at the girl's game, Oona drew a heart in the air and found the girl continuing to copy her.

She stuck out her tongue, the older girl glancing down and discovering her sister doing the same. They began to chuckle, the three of them connected in brief amusement.

'OONA?'

She turned to Dorothy's call, looking over her shoulder. 'Over here,' she responded, seeing a flash of the woman's blue dress between the trees.

Looking back across the stream, she found no trace of the sisters and her smile faded.

'There you are,' said Dotty as she reached the stream a few yards to the left and came to a halt. 'I was getting a little worried, so thought I'd come find you.'

'I'm fine, thank you,' she replied with another glance at the trees on the far bank.

'Do you want to help me find the roots and leaves?' she enquired. 'I've already found a couple,' she added, lifting her right hand, a few green sprigs clasped in her fingers.

Oona nodded and took up her walking stick. Getting to her feet, she hobbled over to Dorothy, who turned and began towards the cottage.

Pausing a moment, she turned to look across the stream one final time. There was no evidence of the girls and she considered the possibility that she'd fallen asleep whilst sitting on the rock, Dorothy's cry waking her from the dream of the Indian visitation.

Shaking her head, she set off after the woman, who kept her pace purposefully slow. Catching up, they walked side by side through the trees as the morning drew on.

Oona found herself seated on the edge of the porch once again, the early afternoon sun high above. Dorothy crouched before her, a bowl in her hand as she looked to the injured ankle. The walking earlier in the day had seen to increasing the swelling, the joint angry with redness.

'You'd better rest up for the remainder of the day,' commented Dotty as she dipped a couple of fingers into the deep green salve in the bowl. 'Brace yourself,' she warned, preparing to apply it.

Oona gritted her teeth. The application was cool, but even the gentle pressure of Dorothy's fingers brought jolts of pain. Her grip on the edge of the boards grew tighter and she winced.

Dotty glanced up, seeing the blush upon the girl's cheeks. 'Not much longer,' she reassured, dipping her fingers in once again and scooping up more of the remedy.

Walter walked out of the forest to the east, pan in hand and britches darkened by moisture. 'Looks worse than it did this morning,' he commented as he drew close. 'You should rest up for the rest of the day.'

'That's just what I was saying,' responded Dorothy, keeping her attention on applying the paste. 'Any luck?'

Walter drew to a halt beside his wife and slipped his free hand into his pocket. Pulling it out, he unfurled his fingers to reveal a small nugget of gold upon his palm. 'A good day,' he stated.

Dorothy glanced at the pea-sized nugget and nodded. 'That's the biggest you've found for a while.'

'Over a year,' he replied, leaning forward so Oona could get a better look, the sun glinting on the precious metal. 'I'll go and add it to the rest,' he stated, moving around them and stepping onto the porch.

'Then you can see to the shingles,' said Dorothy.

'I've got to top up the tables first. We're in need of meat and the squirrels like the pine nuts.'

'And what will your excuse be after that?' she said, pausing and looking up at him with a raised eyebrow.

'I'm not sure yet, but I'm sure I'll think of something,' he answered with a grin, winking at Oona.

She smiled as he turned and entered the cottage. Footsteps marked his passage across the floorboards towards the chimney as Dorothy finished covering the injury with the concoction.

'There,' she stated, sitting back on her haunches, 'all done.' She wiped her fingers on the grass beside her. 'Hopefully, it won't be long until you begin to feel the benefit. That swelling should come down in no time.'

'Much obliged,' replied Oona as she briefly examined the smear of green paste.

'I should wrap it in a piece of cloth,' she said, getting to her feet with the bowl still in hand. 'I won't be a moment.'

Dorothy entered the cottage. Oona put her head back, closing her eyes and feeling the touch of the sun upon her cheeks. The image of the Indian girls came forth and she pondered whether or not they had been a figment of her imagination.

'Here we go,' said Dorothy as she returned, a strip of yellow cotton in her hand.

She crouched before the girl once again and began wrapping the ankle, careful not to make the bind too tight. 'How's that?' she asked.

'Fine,' replied Oona. 'Be there Injuns hereabouts?' she enquired as Dotty secured the cloth.

Dorothy looked up as she finished. 'What causes you to ask?'

She hesitated. 'I thought I saw two girls in the forest this morning, but it could be I were dreaming.'

'There's a few, but they keep to themselves mostly.'

'They were real?'

'Most likely,' replied Dorothy.

'You say you saw Injuns?' Walter walked out onto the porch with the sack of feed at his side.

Oona turned to look over her shoulder and nodded. 'By a stream south of here.'

'I ain't seen any in a long count, though I'd guess they've seen me aplenty. When we first moved here, they'd come by and try to trade furs and the like, but once they found we hadn't got anything worth trading, they stopping coming.'

'Be they peaceful?'

'They ain't never caused us no problems,' replied Walter. 'They're of the Creek Nation. Been here for generations, but most were moved to the reservations. There's only a few holdouts left.'

'Do they live close?'

Walt shrugged. 'I ain't never come across their home,' he stated, stepping down and starting towards the nearest bird table. 'Must be somewhere deep in the forest to the north.'

Oona sat thoughtfully mulling over what he'd said as he tipped some of the feed from the sack onto the table.

Dorothy noted her expression and moved to sit beside her. 'Don't be thinking of going in search of them,' she stated. 'They ain't too partial to strangers sniffing around and you're as likely to come across a bear as you are Injuns.'

'I won't go looking for their home,' said Oona, careful with the wording of her reply, mind already set on visiting the same stream the following morning in the hope of seeing the sisters again.

14

Walter sat carving, working on the wings once again, his tongue poking from between his lips as he concentrated. Dorothy was seated on the floor, the patchwork of furs used in conjunction with the bed cover laid across her lap as she saw to small repairs.

Oona enjoyed the comfort of the second armchair, Dotty having insisted she seat herself there in order to rest her ankle. She'd spent time watching Walt, but declined his offer of a tutorial in the craft.

The flames in the hearth distracted her from thoughts of her life at the plantation. Mesmerised by their movements, her mind was blank, body sunken into the embrace of the chair.

The logs spat and Dorothy looked up to check that an ember hadn't been cast out onto the patchwork. 'You all right?' she asked, noting Oona's faraway look.

She blinked and turned to the woman, nodding in response.

'I'm often entranced by the flames,' said Dotty in understanding.

'Will you be wanting your chair back?' asked Oona.

'I'm just fine here, thank you,' she smiled. 'You need to give that ankle of yours time to heal,' she added with a nod towards the yellow cloth about the joint. 'Besides, there's more room on the floor for me to be about my business.'

Barking arose in the darkness that held sway outside.

Oona sat bolt upright and stared at the closed shutters. 'What were that?' she said, fearful that the hounds of the plantation had finally caught up with her.

'Wolves,' stated Walter, placing the carving on the floor and rising.

He walked over to the window and unfastened the shutters as the women looked on. Opening one side slightly, he peered out.

'See them?' asked Dorothy.

Walter didn't reply immediately, his eyes narrowed as he tried to see if the creatures were in the clearing. Movement to the left caught his attention and he spied the lean silhouettes of two of the beasts. 'There's a pair of them out there,' he said without turning.

Oona got out of the chair and took up her walking stick. Hobbling over, Walter stepped aside and pointed to where the wolves were skirting the clearing.

Taking a moment for her sight to adjust to the moonlit darkness, Oona saw the creatures padding southward. 'They be smaller than I thought,' she commented.

'These are red wolves,' responded Walter. 'They're smaller and less ferocious than the greys. We ain't never had any trouble from them. It's the bears you have to watch out for.'

Oona watched as they vanished from sight between the trunks. Stepping away from the window, Walter closed the shutters as she made her way back to the armchair.

'Both are good enough reason not to go wandering after dark,' stated Dorothy as she returned her attention to the sewing. 'It may be we should bring the pail back inside.'

'I'll see to it after I'm done with the wings,' responded her husband as he went to a jug of water on the table at the rear and poured some into a tin cup.

Oona retook her seat, leaning the stick against the arm. Her initial shock sank away in the warm embrace of the chair, but her thoughts were not so easily dismissed.

She considered the possibility that she was still hunted. Her ownership papers stated that she was the property of her master, but now that he was dead, she wondered what lengths would be taken to retrieve her.

Sighing, she thought that lawmen would likely be keen to discover her whereabouts. If they did, her future would hold a rope and sharp drop.

'What are you thinking about?' asked Dorothy as Walter seated himself and picked up the carving.

'Nothing,' replied Oona, glancing down before turning her gaze to the flames once again, hoping they'd have the same distracting effect as earlier.

15

Oona watched from the porch as Walter and Dorothy headed east. They passed into the trees, the former carrying his pan and his wife a basket of washing. The sun was already above the trees, its warmth a welcome tonic after a night disturbed by nightmares relating to her past.

Leaning forward, she looked down at her ankle. The swelling had reduced so much overnight that the cloth Dorothy had tied about it had slipped from place as she tossed and turned. She'd removed it upon rising, finding the skin less inflamed and the pain minimal.

Taking up the walking stick from beside her and looking to the trees to check the couple were out of sight, Oona got to her feet. She stepped onto the porch and closed the door before setting off across the clearing.

Glancing at the bird tables as she passed, she found that more than half of what Walter had placed on them the previous day had been devoured. 'Must have been birds,' she mumbled, recalling that he'd stood at the window for a good couple of hours at the end of day with his crossbow, seeing neither hide nor hair of a squirrel.

Entering the woodland, the air temperature dropped a few degrees, the night's chill still lingering beneath the boughs. Sniffing, the end of her nose cold, Oona listened for the stream, knowing that it wasn't far from the cottage.

Reaching its narrow flow, she sought out the rock upon which she'd sat the previous day. She made her way upstream, spying it ten yards ahead. Limping along the bank and avoiding roots that rose from the rich soil, she went to the boulder and gratefully seated herself.

Looking up, she sought out the sun, letting its rays rest upon her face as they pierced the branches above. With occasional glances into the forest on the far side, she waited, hopeful that the sisters would make another appearance.

Time meandered slowly and she became increasingly convinced that they would not come. She picked at moss on the side of the rock and watched a small spider move away from the disturbance.

A song that Etty had sung to her came to mind. It had often been used as a lullaby after bad dreams, spoken lyrically and softly, Etty's sonorous tones adding to its calming effect.

'The spring, it brings new birth,' began Oona. 'The earth a song of joy, I sing in praise of You, for I'll be coming home.

'The summer, it brings the heat, the beat of the blazing sun, to ripen the harvest of the soul, for I'll be coming home.

'The fall, it brings the reaping, the weeping of tree and sky, soft farewells and fading light, for I'll be coming home.

'The winter, it brings the sleep, the deep snows that cover all, in the death that ain't truly so, for I'll be coming home to You, oh Lord, for I'll be coming home.'

She took a deep breath, tears in her eyes. 'Thank you, Etty,' she whispered, glancing up and the sunlight lending her tears a golden hue.

Blinking, she looked around, finding no sign of the sisters. 'They ain't coming and I need to be back before Dotty returns,' she stated, sighing and taking up her stick.

Standing, her shoulders slumped with disappointment, Oona made her way north through the trunks.

16

Walter stood at the open window, the light fading fast. The crossbow rested on the sill as he stared out at the bird tables. 'Not a one,' he grumbled without turning.

'That's the second day in a row,' commented Dorothy as she stood at the table, chopping board before her, knife in one hand and pale carrot in the other. 'Lucky I went foraging earlier.'

Oona got up from Dotty's chair and added a log to the young fire.

Dorothy noted her actions and looked over to her husband. 'I think it's time to give up and get that window closed. It's starting to get chilly in here.'

Walter sighed. Stepping to the right, he leant the weapon beside the quiver, leaving it loaded.

Going back to the window, he closed the shutters with a frown. 'I don't know what's keeping them away,' he stated, making his way over to his armchair.

'You standing there with a deadly weapon in your hands, I shouldn't wonder,' responded Dorothy as she chopped the vegetables for the broth.

His frown deepened, not amused by her comment. He rubbed his brow and glanced over at the carving of the bird that he'd been working on, finding no motivation to continue.

'If you're at a loose end, you could be fetching some water in,' said Dorothy with a glance at the back of her husband's head as he reclined.

'I've just sat down,' he said with irritation.

'Well, ain't you the lucky one. I'm still on my feet and preparing supper for us all.'

'I'll go,' offered Oona.

'Thank you, Sweetie, but what with those wolves last night and your healing ankle, it'd be best if Walt headed out.'

'She's right,' he conceded, pushing up off the arms and making for the back of the room.

He went to stand beside his wife and crouched, pulling a bucket out from beneath the table. The last of the clean water splashed in the bottom as he took hold of the handle and straightened.

'If I'm not back in good time, send out a search party,' he commented dryly as he went to the door and passed out of the cottage.

'Pay him no mind. Walt can get a bit ornery sometimes,' said Dorothy, glancing over at Oona. 'Sorry there's no meat for supper.'

'It don't matter,' she replied with a thin smile. 'Can I be helping you with the vegetables?'

Dorothy shook her head. 'It's all in hand, thank you. I'm going to add the root leftover from what we collected yesterday. It may be that'll give it a little more flavour.'

She turned her attention to the chopping and they fell into silence. Oona got up and took a couple more logs from the woodpile, adding them to the fire.

Seating herself on the edge of the chair, she held her hands to the flames, the chill that had been let in through the open window starting to be chased away now that the shutters were closed. The fire spat an ember, which hit the boards and sent orange sparks skittering across the floor. They blackened and died, becoming specks of soot upon the wood.

Oona looked at them reflectively, feeling melancholia rising at the sight. 'Life be but a brief light,' she mumbled.

'Did you say something?' asked Dorothy.

'I just be talking to myself,' she replied over the back of the chair.

Boots sounded on the porch.

'That were quick,' stated Dotty as they both turned to the door in expectation of Walter's entrance.

Two knocks followed and Oona glanced at Dotty curiously.

'Hide yourself,' instructed the woman in an urgent whisper.

Oona got up, taking hold of her stick and glancing around the room. 'Where?'

'Under the bed covers,' replied Dorothy, pointing to the cot in the shadows of the far corner.

Oona made her way as quickly as she could, conscious of the tapping of her walking stick. Dotty went towards the door, holding the chopping knife with a tightening grip.

Waiting until the girl had climbed beneath the covers and hidden herself as best she could, Dorothy took hold of the handle and opened the door. A middle-aged man stood on the threshold, his long dark hair matted and tangled. He had an unkempt beard and a desperate look to his brown eyes. His clothes were dirt stained and bedraggled, a few cooking utensils tied to the pack on his back.

'Can you spare any food?' he asked in a hoarse voice, cheekbones protruding and skin sunken beneath. 'Maybe shelter for the night?'

'What are you doing in the forest?' she asked, catching the scent of his body on the light breeze.

'I lost my job and my home in Kansas City,' he replied. 'I'd heard there was gold out here and came to find my fortune.'

'It don't look like you've found much of anything.'

'Just stones and dirt.'

'It's been a good count of years since the gold rush.'

His stomach groaned loudly and he glanced over her shoulder, looking to the chopped vegetables and cooking pot that Dorothy had placed nearby. 'Will you take pity on a weary traveller?'

'Who are you then?' asked Walter as he materialised from the darkness of the forest, bucket at his side pulling his arm straight with its weight.

The young man turned. 'Good evening, Sir. I were just speaking with your…' He glanced back at Dorothy. '…Daughter,' he finished with uncertainty.

Walter's expression soured slightly. 'Wife,' he corrected as he drew near.

'My apologies. The light ain't so good,' responded the man. 'I was asking if I can stay the night and partake in supper.'

Walter looked at Dorothy, a question in his expression. She glanced towards the bed while the man's back was turned and he gave a shallow nod.

'We can't be putting you up,' said Walt, 'but it may be we can give you a little food before you're on your way.'

'That would be a kindness.'

'What name do you go by?'

'Ethan. Ethan O'Callaghan. My father was Irish.'

'I'm Walt and this here is Dotty,' he introduced, holding his hand towards his wife as she remained in the doorway. 'She'll fetch out some food.'

'Can I come in and find warmth before your fire.'

There was a sneeze from inside. Dorothy turned to the bed, Ethan leaning forward and peering around the doorframe.

'Who's that?' he enquired.

Dotty looked to her husband.

'Our daughter,' stated Walter. 'She's sickly and we don't want her disturbed or anyone catching what ails her.'

'You know what she's got?' asked Ethan, stepping back to the edge of the porch.

Walt shook his head. 'But whatever it is, it ain't pleasant,' he replied, seeing the stranger's increased nervousness and hoping to discourage him further. 'Anyone with a weak constitution would be well advised to steer clear.'

Oona sneezed again as she remained hidden beneath the covers, sniffing loudly afterwards to add weight to Walter's lie.

'I'll get you some food,' stated Dorothy, turning away.

Ethan held up his hands. 'I'll be just fine,' he responded, shaking his head and moving off the porch, worried the food would be contaminated. 'I've got a little in my pack and can set a trap for some meat.'

'You sure?' asked Dotty.

He nodded. 'Sorry to have disturbed you.' He turned and began to walk southward, glancing at the bird tables that he passed and cooking utensils clanking against each other with each stride.

Walter and Dorothy watched him leave, seeing his shadowy form enter the tree line.

'You'd better come in,' she said, stepping aside.

Walter walked in with the bucket of water and she closed the door, putting a hand to her chest and taking a deep breath.

'That was quick thinking.'

'You didn't just marry me for my looks,' replied her husband, walking to the rear of the room and placing the bucket on the floor by the table as Oona pulled back the cover and sat up.

'Sorry,' she said miserably. 'Dust were tickling my nose.'

'It ain't your fault,' responded Dorothy, walking over to seat herself on the edge of the cot. 'Besides, you gave the excuse to send him on his way.'

'By accident.'

'Nonetheless.' She reached out and took Oona's hand. 'You're safe from discovery.'

Dorothy's expression dropped, face filled with shadows cast by the fire at her back.

'What be wrong?' enquired Oona with concern.

Dotty looked to the girl's eyes and placed her free hand to her cheek. 'It's a shame we have to worry about your discovery at all. I would that it were a more accepting world.'

'Maybe one day,' replied Oona.

'Maybe one day,' echoed Dorothy with a nod. 'I'd best get to finishing supper.' She squeezed the girl's hand before releasing it and rising from the bed.

Walter's stomach grumbled. 'My belly's in agreement,' he commented, trying to lighten the mood as he patted it.

'Your belly is always in want of food,' responded Dorothy, going to the table to gather up the chopped vegetables and throw them in the pot.

17

Oona bathed in an eddy created by a half-moon of rocks at the edge of the creek. The water was cold, its chill contrasting with the sun's warmth upon her bare shoulders. She ducked her head beneath after taking a breath, running her hands over her face and head.

Breaking the surface, she blinked to clear her vision and looked up at the pines. They moved in the wind and she noted clusters of cones, along with the vibrant green of new growth. A squirrel came into view, scampering along one of the nearest branches.

The tickle of water on her nose caused her to sneeze. The creature immediately turned and fled. It ran along the bough to the trunk and passed around to the far side before making the climb. She tried to locate it, narrowing her eyes and catching glimpses before it neared the top and leapt to another tree further from the creek.

'You'd best be staying away from the cottage,' she warned, 'Walter ain't shot anything for days and we're in need of meat.'

Spending a few more moments in the water, she reached for her stick resting on the bankside rocks. Holding the knotted end in both hands, it bent as it took her weight and she hauled herself up.

She placed her injured foot to the bed of the creek and leant on it a little. There was no pain. Adding greater pressure, she found it much better than before and was thankful for both the rest and the curative that Dorothy had provided.

'It won't be too long before I can be walking without the stick,' she commented, smiling to herself.

She limped to the side of the pool created by the rocks. Temporarily setting the branch down, she pulled herself out and got to her feet once again. Her clothes lay on a large boulder nearby, set out in the sun.

Oona dressed in contented silence, the warmth of the garments pleasing upon her skin. Once finished, she bent for the stick and readied herself for the return journey to the cottage, glancing about the creek.

A bee came buzzing about. She remained still and watched as it occasioned the wildflowers upon the bank beyond the rocks.

'New life,' she stated, eyes glistening as she was overcome by a swell of joy. She hadn't thought to find such contentment, one coupled with a freedom she'd never dreamt of.

The image of the razor in her hand vanquished her brief ecstasy in an instant. 'I don't be deserving this life,' she said, shoulders dropping as she looked to the sky.

'Be that my punishment? To be in Eden and know I don't belong?' she asked, 'or be it to taste such a life only to have it stolen away?'

The birds sang and the trees whispered as the waters burbled past, but no answer was forthcoming.

'It may be that my sin will condemn those who harbour me,' she added, suddenly worried that her presence was a blight that would infect the souls of the kindly couple who'd taken her in. 'Surely You would not judge them for my sins when they don't be knowing what I done?'

The sounds of the forest remained the only reply to her enquiries.

With a frustrated sign, she set off towards the cottage, making her way into the trees. Recalling the elation she had so recently felt, she tried to push away the dark thoughts that had overshadowed it.

'What did Etty once say?' she mumbled to herself, a fragment of memory coming to her. She had been crying upon her bed in the bunkhouse. It was after one of the occasions she was hung in the meat locker, her wrists bleeding and clutched to her chest as she lay balled on her side.

She'd come to believe the Lord was punishing her, that the life she found herself living was divinely ordained. She could think of no great sin that she'd committed and had come to the conclusion that to warrant such a terrible sentence, she must be rotten inside.

Etty had found her distraught and filled with torment. Sitting on the bed and gathering her into her arms, she'd stroked her cheeks and comforted her.

Oona came to a halt amidst the pines, suddenly recollecting what the old slave had said when she'd discovered what was afflicting her. 'Joy, love, forgiveness; such things are of God,' she began. 'If you give them, you are doing His work. If you feel them, you are touched by the Lord Himself.'

Bowing her head as she recalled the joy she'd felt only minutes before, Oona wept as the trees looked on.

'Thank you,' she said with a sniffle, glancing to the sky.

18

Oona limped into the clearing, her eyes raw from crying. A few birds fluttered to branches, their foraging at the tables disturbed by her arrival.

She walked towards the cottage, the door and window open on the mild day, but no sign of the couple. She hoped that they were in residence, longed for company after her solitary tears.

As she drew closer, she could hear the murmur of their voices within. The words grew more distinct as she neared the porch, coming to a standstill a few yards shy of the window.

'So, what we going to do about Oona?' asked Walter.

'As I've already said, let's wait and see,' replied Dorothy, her tone one of annoyance.

'Wait for what? We may as well decide now.'

'I'm not deciding anything, I'm cooking.'

'And you can't think and cook?' replied Walt sarcastically.

'I'll tell you what I'm thinking; I'm thinking that my husband should take more care how he speaks to me.'

Chopping arose from inside the house, loud and exaggerated by annoyance.

'I'll hear no more of it and, if your wisdom has grown with your age, you'll know when to hold your tongue,' said Dorothy, the sound of blade against board continuing as she spoke.

Oona heard footsteps approaching the front door. Turning, she made for the corner of the house. Reaching it before Walter appeared in the entrance, she stifled a cry of pain as she fell to the ground after placing too much weight on her injured ankle.

Walt stepped from the porch with the feed sack in hand. His attention elsewhere and with a quickness to his steps that hinted at his frustration after the conversation with his wife, he made for the nearest table.

She watched his agitated movements as he took a handful of the food and threw it onto the wood, a few grains falling over the sides. His back to her as he went to the next feeder, she quietly got to her feet and began alongside the house, passing about the chimney stack.

Moving with as much haste as she could, Oona made for the trees north of the clearing, hampered by the renewed throbbing in her foot.

'Oona? I thought you were to the creek.'

She came to a halt, shoulders tightening. She turned to find Walter regarding her closely, having moved to a feeder on the western side of the house. 'I've done washed,' she stated.

'Where you off to now? Ain't you coming in for lunch?' he asked, detecting stiffness in her expression and posture. 'Dotty's preparing it in readiness for your return.'

She tried to think of a plausible explanation. 'I left something on the bank.'

His brow furrowed, her direction of travel not fitting with her reply. 'What's wrong, Oona?' he enquired.

'Nothing.'

'Well, for someone who says nothing's wrong, you sure are acting queer. You're also headed in the wrong direction for the creek,' he stated.

She glanced at the trees behind her, longing for their cover but knowing that she had no chance of escape due to her injury. 'I done heard what you were talking about in the house,' she stated, deciding her only option was to confront the man.

Walter looked at her in confusion. 'I don't know what you mean.'

'You was deciding my fate.'

'Oh, that,' he responded with a gentle smile of relief, expression softening. 'I'm happy to say, you've got it all wrong, Oona.'

'I heard you clear as day.'

'Yes, you heard us, but it honestly ain't what you think,' he said. 'We were talking about what we'll tell Ezra when he comes a calling. It ain't a common thing to visit with your parents and find a negro in residence.'

'What you'll tell Ezra?'

'Our son. He's due to visit soon and, well…' His smile faded. '…He ain't quite as friendly as we are, if you catch my drift.'

She nodded. 'You want I should go?'

'We want you to stay,' he replied without hesitation, 'but we also need to think of something to tell Ezra.'

Oona could detect no deceit, though remained guarded. 'I could hide when he comes.'

'That's not what we want.'

'Or stay at the creek until he's been. There be a hollow…'

'No,' said Walter, cutting her off. 'There's no need. We'll arrive at some story to tell. It may be you will have to play a part for the duration of his stay,' he added, unable to hold her gaze when he said the last.

'A part?'

He sighed. 'As our slave,' he stated regretfully.

Oona stared at him a moment. 'I understand,' she said quietly, a despondent look upon her young face.

'You talking to yourself again?' Dorothy's enquiry arose from behind Walter.

He looked over his shoulder. 'I'm talking to Oona.'

'What's wrong?' she asked as she approached, noting his downcast expression and glancing at the girl as she lingered near the tree line.

'I told her what we'd been speaking about inside,' he stated.

Dorothy looked at him without comprehension.

'About when Ezra comes a calling,' he clarified.

Realisation dawned. 'Why'd you go and spill that when we ain't even decided on what to do?' she asked in annoyance.

'She overheard us and mistook our meaning.'

Dorothy looked to the girl. 'We were only talking about what to say to our son,' she stated, underlining what her husband had already said.

Oona nodded, but made no reply.

Dorothy walked towards her with her hands out and a sad look upon her face. 'We mean no harm or hurt. We just want you to be safe, and that means concocting a story that'll keep you so.' Her words were filled with sincerity and her eyes with concern as she neared the girl.

Coming to a halt, she reached for Oona's free hand and took it in both of hers, holding it tight. 'We would protect you and see to your safety,' she said softly. 'Come inside, lunch is waiting.'

Oona nodded once again, unable to speak for fear of releasing the emotions that churned inside.

Holding Oona's hand, Dorothy led her back to the cottage, Walter falling into step behind after they'd passed him by.

19

The dusk was thickened by heavy rain, strengthening winds having brought low cloud to blanket the end of day. Oona sat cross-legged before the fire with a bowl in one hand and spoon in the other, Walter and Dorothy seated in their chairs behind the girl.

She collected up the last of the vegetable soup, glancing into the hearth at the hiss of water falling from the chimney. Swallowing and setting down the spoon, she took up a piece of flatbread balanced upon her knee. Wiping it around the inside, she mopped up the residue and placed the bread into her mouth.

Oona put the bowl on the boards beside her and sighed, staring at the flames towards the rear of the grate as they struggled against the dripping rainwater. Each time a drop fell, their vigour was diminished, only to return an instant later.

The atmosphere was subdued by what had occurred earlier and the change in weather, but she had no wish to lighten it. It suited her mood; melancholia having settled its darkness upon her heart.

'Would you like more?' asked Walter as he pushed up from his seat and stepped to the pot hanging above the fire.

'No, thank you,' she replied without looking.

'How's your ankle?' asked Dorothy, resting her bowl upon her lap after drinking the dregs.

'Throbbing,' responded Oona simply.

Walter retook his seat, the couple glancing at each other meaningfully.

'I hope what we said ain't upset you,' he said, taking up his spoon as Dotty got up and went to the cabinet beside the table.

Oona shook her head. 'Just tired.'

'You sure?' he pursued, his wife bringing him a fresh piece of flatbread and placing it on the arm of his chair. He touched her hand in thanks before she seated herself once more.

'It may be the weather effects my mood,' she added.

'It'll blow over by morning,' said Dorothy. 'As long as it does, there's something I'd like to show you.'

Oona looked back at her. 'What?'

'If I tell you, it'll ruin the surprise.' She adopted a stiff smile.

The girl regarded her for a while longer and then turned back to the fire. 'Should I put more logs on?'

'May as well let it burn out. It won't be long until we're to our beds,' replied Dorothy. 'I hope the pillow is serving you well,' she added, glancing at Oona's small sleeping space in the corner.

She nodded her response.

Dotty sighed and looked to her husband again. Walt shrugged as he ate another spoonful of soup.

Slipping from the chair, Dorothy went to sit beside the girl, adopting the same posture with the crack of her knees. 'It's like they're dancing with the joy of life,' she said, staring at the flames.

'Or writhing in pain,' responded Oona darkly.

'No, it's a dance, sure enough.'

'Dancing over the ashes of what they've done consumed.'

Dotty frowned and turned to study the girl's profile. 'You sure there ain't more to your mood than weariness and weather?' she asked, placing her hand upon the girl's knee.

Oona looked at the woman's pale fingers upon her dress. 'It be as I said,' she reiterated, her gaze returning to the flames.

Dorothy removed her hand after noting the glance. Knitting her fingers upon her lap, she tried to think of more to say, seeking some topic of conversation that may lift the girl from the dark mood that consumed her.

'Anyone want more or can I finish it off?'

'You want thirds again?' asked Dorothy, turning to her husband. 'Ain't your belly full yet or have you got worms?'

'I've always been partial to your mushroom soup,' he replied.

'You'll be fit to pop,' she said, turning to Oona. 'When we go to our bed, the darn thing will collapse under the weight,' she joked.

The girl didn't respond.

A bang and clatter arose against the front wall. They all turned to the brief commotion as the rain drummed on the roof and the wind buffeted the cottage.

'Sounds like more of the porch roof has come away,' stated Walter as he got up to serve himself.

'If you'd have fixed it like I told you, then it would have likely held fast,' responded Dorothy, all amusement absent from her tone, the girl's mood lowering her spirits.

Walt made no reply as he ladled what remained of the soup into his bowl. The metal implement scraped against the sides and Dotty stared at the back of his head, biting back a comment.

Returning to his seat, Walter settled himself and set about eating the final portion. The cottage filled with the sounds of the squall that engulfed it, Oona conducting a silent vigil as the flames in the fireplace slowly died and writhed in the numerous drafts passing about the room.

20

A solitary lamp lit the study as it rested on the writing desk. James Woodruff sat behind with his back to the darkened window, papers held in his skeletal hands as he scanned the uppermost with narrowed eyes. His thin lips moved as he read, a drooping moustache flecked with grey partially hiding the activity. A monocle rested beside him despite his obvious need of its magnification and a pipe lay with its bowl in an ashtray nearby. To his right was a bell set on a small silver tray, a distorted reflection of the room in its polished curves.

Footsteps drew his gaze to the door on the right. Two sharp knocks followed.

'Come,' he responded, lowering the papers.

His head house slave entered with a dutiful bow. 'The two gentlemen you sent for are at the door, Master.'

'See them up, Moses.'

'As you wish.' Moses backed out of the room, closing the door after him.

Woodruff rested the papers on the desk. Taking up his pipe, he reclined against the back of the chair. He crossed his legs and took a pouch of tobacco from the pocket of his suit jacket, proceeding to stuff the bowl.

Three sets of steps came up the stairs in the grand hall and walked along the curved landing. Woodruff adopted a commanding posture. Placing the pipe to his lips, he lit a match as the footsteps came to halt before the door and Moses knocked for a second time.

He inhaled and tossed the spent match into the ashtray. 'You may enter,' he breathed, releasing a plume of smoke.

Moses opened the door and stepped into the room, moving aside so the pair of bounty hunters could enter, pistols holstered at their hips.

'Mr John Wallace and Felix Fitch,' he announced.

'Leave us,' instructed Woodruff, sucking on his pipe.

'Yes, Master.' Moses bowed and left the room.

The men walked over to the desk, leather britches dusted by the road.

'I'm Wallace,' introduced the taller man, clasping his brown Stetson and holding out his free hand.

Woodruff stared at it, noting grime beneath the nails and shaking his head in refusal. 'Are you aware of my reason for summoning you here?'

'Summoning?' Fitch raised an eyebrow and glanced up at his companion, the collar of his brown jacket raised, black hair and beard unkempt.

'Yes, summoning,' confirmed Woodruff sternly. 'You are men seeking employment and I am the man seeking to employ you.'

'If you've a slave that's hightailed it out of here, then we're the right men for the job,' stated Wallace. 'Ain't a one that's eluded us in five years.'

'Six,' corrected Fitch.

'This one's slippery,' said Woodruff, remaining perfectly still as he sat straight-backed in the upholstered chair, the rivets creating a cold silver border that accentuated the darkness of his suit. 'She evaded my men and the hounds.'

'We've come across the same before,' said Fitch, scratching the side of his bulbous nose. 'Ain't no one can track as good as me.'

Woodruff didn't spare Felix a glance as he filled his lungs with smoke. 'I hear your services come at a fair price,' he exhaled.

'Fair and honest,' nodded Wallace.

He opened the bottom drawer and took out a monogrammed black velvet pouch. Reaching out and setting it on the desk before Wallace, the chink of coins could be heard within. 'This is what I am paying you to bring her back.'

'We've the same initials,' observed Wallace, noting the letters in white stitching as he picked the pouch up and pulled open the drawstrings, peering inside.

'I can assure you, that is all we have in common,' responded Woodruff, taking another drag on the pipe.

'This ain't enough.' Wallace lifted his gaze.

'Half now, half upon delivery.'

'What of unforeseen expenses?' asked Fitch.

'What of them?' Woodruff turned to him.

'It'll be enough,' stated Wallace, making to put the pouch into the pocket of his tan jacket.

'The pouch is not part of the payment.'

Wallace put the top of the pouch into his pocket and tipped the coins in. 'Who we looking for?' he enquired as he placed the velvet bag onto the desk before him.

'A girl,' stated Woodruff, reaching forward and collecting it before settling back against the chair and drawing on his pipe. 'She's thirteen and goes by the name of Oona Mae.'

'Thirteen,' snorted Fitch. 'And you say your men couldn't find her?' he added derisively.

Woodruff stiffened, expression hardening and smoke coiling from his thin nostrils. 'She slit my brother's throat,' he stated, glaring at the stout man.

'How long since she ran?' asked Wallace, wishing to dispel the sudden tension.

'Five days,' replied Woodruff, turning back to the taller man.

'Five days!' exclaimed Fitch. 'The trail will likely be as cold as a nun's cooch.'

'If you'd have come when the rider first delivered my message, it would have been two days,' responded Woodruff coldly as he turned his gaze to Fitch once again.

'We were finishing a job near Macon,' explained Wallace. 'You know which direction she went?'

'East,' replied Woodruff, glaring at the other slave hunter as if daring him to offer further complaint.

'Do you want her brought back alive?'

'Yes,' he replied. 'I want to see her hang for what she did.'

He took the pipe from his mouth and tapped the rim of the bowl on the edge of the ashtray. Setting it down in the receptacle, he picked up the bell and rang it with practiced sharpness.

'Our business here is concluded,' announced Woodruff. 'Good day to you,' he added dismissively, putting the empty pouch back into the bottom drawer and lifting the papers he'd been examining earlier.

Wallace and Fitch glanced at each other as their new employer began to leaf through the paperwork. The door to the study opened and Moses stepped in.

'See these *gentlemen* to the door,' he instructed with open disdain.

Moses stepped back and held out his arm to indicate that the guests should make their way from the study.

'I said, good day,' reiterated Woodruff, not deigning to lift his gaze.

'There's one last thing,' said Fitch.

Woodruff let out an impatient sigh as he looked up at the bounty hunter.

'I get to take one of her teeth.' He opened the top buttons of the pale shirt that he wore beneath his black jacket, revealing a cord of leather about his neck strung with incisors. 'There's one for each slave we've hunted down.'

Glancing at the necklace distastefully, Woodruff turned his gaze back to the papers. 'Agreed,' he stated. 'Now, I have other business to attend to.' He waved them away with a condescending flick of his hand.

With another shared look, Wallace led the way out of the room.

'Not as cordial as we're used to,' commented Fitch, purposefully keeping his voice loud enough for Woodruff to hear.

Moses dutifully closed the door behind the bounty hunters and began to lead them along the extravagant landing to the stairs. Woodruff looked to the door, lowering the papers. His expression stern, he picked up his pipe and delved into his pocket for the tobacco pouch.

'Your days are numbered, Oona Mae,' he mumbled as he stuffed weed into the bowl.

21

Oona opened her eyes to the darkness. Reaching forward, she discovered she was facing the wall when her fingers came into contact with the slats. She frowned as she looked to the shutters, unable to see them, but hearing them bump against the frame. It had taken quite some time to fall asleep due to the cacophony unleashed by the wind and rain and she'd woken several times already, each time shifting to a new position and trying to settle again.

She yawned and tears were forced from her eyes. Rolling onto her back, the hairs on the nape of her neck prickled when she detected a presence.

Swallowing against rising fear, she tried to discern the cause of the sensation, staring at the thick dark within the cottage in the hope it would reveal its secrets.

Oona heard shallow breathing nearby and went still, an icy shiver passing the length of her spine. Looking up, she thought she could detect the vague shape of someone standing by her sleeping area.

'Dotty? Walt?' she whispered, heart pounding and breath stolen by the tightness of her chest.

The floorboards creaked as whoever stood over her shifted slightly.

'Who's there?'

Still no response came.

Disturbance arose from the bed in the far corner.

'Walter?' Dorothy's enquiry was partially concealed by the rain.

Oona listened as the woman got out of bed and padded across to the table. A drawer opened. Shortly after, a match flared and Walter was revealed standing as if transfixed, arms at his sides.

The flame was taken to a candle in a blackened holder, Dorothy taking the handle and turning to scan the interior. Setting eyes on her husband and the scared girl before him, she hurried over, the candlelight flickering and projecting shadows that danced upon the walls.

She came to a halt beside Walter and bent forward to look at his face, his eyes open but staring straight ahead. 'I'm so sorry,' she stated, crouching and putting a hand to Oona's shoulder. 'I should have warned you of this.'

'What be his affliction?' asked the girl, trying to calm herself.

'He wanders in his sleep on occasion, and always when the wind howls through the trees. It's as if it calls to him.' Dorothy glanced up at her husband.

'Shouldn't we be waking him?' asked Oona, following her gaze.

She shook her head. 'I only tried once and never again. He screamed like the greatest horror had befallen him, but would not wake. Now I just leave him to come round as nature intended.'

'Will he stand there all night?' Oona turned her worried gaze back to the woman.

She smiled disarmingly. 'Don't worry, you can sleep with me,' she said, squeezing the girl's shoulder.

'Truly?'

'Ain't no harm in comforting the distressed, like a mother comforting a child,' she replied, taking hold of Oona's hand as the flame fluttered.

She encouraged the girl to her feet and they stepped past Walter as he remained eerily still. Going over to the bed, Dorothy put the candle on the floor beside.

'You'd better get in first, just in case Walt returns,' she said, pulling the covers back.

Oona climbed in, feeling the weight of the patchwork of furs as she moved to the far side.

'Would you like me to leave the candle burning?'

The girl shook her head, the gesture undermined by the fretful expression upon her face.

'You sure?'

'Yes,' stated Oona, trying to be brave.

Dorothy got into the bed and leant over the side to blow the flame out. She sidled up next to the girl, drawing her close and placing her arm about her. 'Sleep well, Oona,' she whispered.

The feel and smell of the woman gave her reassurance and she was reminded of the nights she'd spent sleeping with Etty in the bunkhouse. She smiled sadly as she snuggled closer, seeking out Dorothy's warmth.

The image of her master drew out of the darkness behind her lids, triggered by Walter's presence beside her sleeping area. He stood by her cot in the bunkhouse and she knew his intention. He visited the slave quarters regularly, choosing which female would be used to gratify his urges on any particular night. She would lie motionless in her bed waiting for him to make his choice, praying to the Lord that it would not be her and at once feeling guilty that she should wish his loveless attentions upon one of the other slaves.

She quivered and Dorothy held her tighter, mistaking the tremor for coldness. In the pitch black they cuddled together waiting for sleep or the dawn light to release them from the night.

22

Wallace and Fitch drew out of the darkness that was being ushered west by the break of day. They rode slowly along the track towards a trading post nestled in the pines, a lantern above the entrance.

Bringing their horses to a halt outside, they dismounted and walked to the door, Wallace entering first. Another lantern rested on the counter to the right, illuminating an assortment of goods arrayed haphazardly about the small store. The air was made hazy by steam and water could be heard splashing to the rear.

'I'll poke about in here. You check out back,' instructed Wallace, looking at the untidy shelves and assorted items hanging from the posts.

Fitch nodded, walking towards a door beyond the far end of the counter, hand moving to the gun at his hip. He trod softly, gaze set on the portal as occasional splashes arose from beyond. A herbal smell was woven into the light steam and he guessed the proprietor to be bathing.

He took hold of the handle and opened it quickly, ready to draw the pistol. The small back room was swamped with mist. Amidst the paleness was a tin bath, a bearded old man and young Indian squaw engaged in carnal activity within.

The man looked at Fitch in surprise. The squaw ceased her activities as she sat astride him and looked over her shoulder, a scar running along the side of her face and damp hair lying halfway down her back.

'You open for business?' asked Fitch, hand remaining at his holster.

'If you give me a minute, I'll be right with you,' croaked the old man.

Fitch scanned the room and nodded. Retreating, he left the door ajar, hearing the proprietor get out the bath behind. 'Anything?' he asked, looking to Wallace as he lurked in the shadows at the rear, obscured by artefacts hung from one of the posts.

'Nothing,' responded Wallace as he walked over.

The old man made a hasty entrance, white hairs upon his flabby chest and a towel about his waist, his paunch hanging over. His legs were bowed, lending him a metronomic gait as he moved to stand behind the counter.

'The name's Elijah Gray. How can I help you gentlemen?' he enquired, adopting a cordial air despite his state of undress.

'We're looking for a nigger gal,' stated Wallace.

'I'm afraid I ain't to selling the like in here. I got plenty of supplies, but no niggers for sale.'

'You mistake me. We're after a runaway, thirteen and by the name Oona Mae. You seen the like?'

Elijah shook his head. 'Can't say that I have. Don't get many by here since the gold rush days and I remember every face. Ain't seen a black one for a good long time.'

'Only a red one,' commented Fitch with an unkind smile.

'You gentlemen need anything else?' responded Elijah, letting the remark pass. 'I got some darn good whisky here behind the counter,' he added, looking to the bottles on the shelving at his back.

'We'll take one, and some horse feed, if you've got some.'

The old man nodded. 'You fellers slave hunters?' he asked conversationally as he turned his back to them and fetched down a bottle.

'Yes,' replied Wallace. 'You see or hear anything about this girl, you be sure to be remembering just in case we come by again.'

Elijah placed the bottle on the counter. 'Much reward money in it?' he asked with a sparkle in his eyes.

'None for you, old timer,' said Fitch. 'Your reward will be your life.' He rested his hand on his gun.

Elijah glanced at the weapon. 'I'm a peaceable man,' he stated, raising his hands submissively.

'And long may it stay that way,' grinned Fitch.

'Horse feed,' prompted Wallace.

'It's out in the shed,' replied Elijah.

'Then I suggest you go get it,' said Fitch.

'If I take payment first, then you fellers can be on your way without delay,' responded the old man, unable to hide his growing agitation as he wrung his hands.

'Put it on our slate.'

'Your slate?' He looked at Fitch nervously.

'We'll pay it next time we pass this way, but if we find you ain't been truthful you'll be paying a much larger slate.'

'Here.' Wallace tossed a couple of coins on the counter. 'This'll cover it.'

Elijah looked at the coins and then at Wallace with open relief. 'Much obliged,' he said as he gathered them up and slipped them into a lidded tin behind a set of large black scales.

'Take another whisky as a gesture of my goodwill.' He turned to the shelving and took down a second bottle.

Wallace nodded his thanks as he took the bottles from the counter.

'You mark my words, that'll sure warm the cockles on cold nights,' said Elijah with a forced smile.

He shuffled from behind the counter, making for the entrance. 'If you'd care to follow me, I'll take you round to the shed.'

'Maybe I'll wait here and take a dip,' said Fitch with a meaningful glance towards the door at the rear.

Wallace gave his companion a gentle nudge in the back.

'Just having fun,' responded Fitch as they fell into step behind the swaying old man, going out into the waxing day.

23

A hush filled the cottage, the wind and rain having passed. Oona raised her head and looked across Dorothy's sleeping form. Walter had returned to the bed sometime in the early hours and lay with his back to them in the morning gloom.

Resting, she savoured the warmth of the woman, who was snoring softly. Thoughts of Etty drifted into her mind and she smiled, face buried against Dorothy's side.

An image came forth that she'd tried to suppress. Her smile vanished and her expression became pinched as she tried to dispel the haunting sight that had possessed her when she stood with razor in hand.

Taking a wavering breath, tears began to dampen her cheeks.

'Oona?'

She shifted her head and looked up, finding Dorothy regarding her with concern.

'What ails you?'

'A memory,' she whispered in reply.

'Your past is behind you and your future is yet before you,' responded Dotty, 'but your present, well, that's in my arms.' She cuddled the girl close and stroked her hair. 'There ain't nothing to fear.'

There was a brief silence as Oona's tears abated.

'You ever lose someone close?' she asked, eyes closed as she savoured the caresses.

Dorothy took a deep breath, the question unanticipated and bringing forth her own pain. 'Yes,' she replied. 'We had a daughter; Elsa. She were taken by a sickness two years passed. Who did you lose?'

'Etty. She were my mother of sorts. She weren't my real mother though,' said Oona. 'She done took me under her wing.'

'What about your real mother?'

'We were taken to auction and she sold to another master when I were but five. I don't even be remembering her face no more.'

'And Etty? Did sickness take her?'

Oona shook her head against Dorothy's side. 'She were…' She took a breath as she struggled to contain her grief. 'She were beaten to death by our master.'

Dotty looked down at the top of the girl's head with a pained expression, filled with sorrow that one so innocent should have experienced such horror. 'You saw this?'

'Yes,' whispered Oona as tears threatened to fall once again. 'She were trying to stop him taking me for his pleasure.' Her body began to tremble as the sight of Etty lying upon the bunkhouse floor filled her mind. Their master stood over her prone form, scratch marks on his cheeks, fists bloodied and a victorious expression lending his lips a cruel sneer. Etty's face was barely recognisable in the lamplight, battered and bloody as she gurgled her final breaths.

Oona began to weep. Dorothy held her tight, feeling the convulsions of the girl's loss, her nightie dampened by tears.

24

'We'll be heading off now, Walt,' called Dorothy, holding Oona's hand as they exited the cottage, a leather bag slung over her shoulder and the girl's walking stick tapping on the boards.

'There won't be any roof left when you finally get round to making the mends,' she added, glancing at the large hole over her head, the wind having ripped more shingles away.

'I'll see to it after topping up the tables,' replied Walter, tipping the bag of seed in his hands and a small pile falling onto the bird table before him.

'Be sure you do,' said Dorothy as she took Oona eastward towards the creek.

They passed into the pines, beams of sunlight dappling the forest floor. Flies flew with the laziness of morning, the chill that had taken hold after the cloud had cleared not yet chased away by the growing heat of day.

Their pace slowed by the girl's ankle, they savoured the after-rain freshness of the woodland as birdsong lifted their hearts. The tears of the early hours were forgotten amidst the natural surroundings, the contact of their hands helping to reinforce their bond.

'Look,' whispered Dorothy, bringing them to a halt and pointing through the widely spaced trees.

Thirty yards ahead, a small herd of deer were strolling through a pool of sunlight, their flanks golden. Oona stared at them, wondering if they were the same creatures she'd come upon previously.

Continuing on their way, the herd soon vanished from sight in the halls of the forest.

'Does Walt ever kill deer with his crossbow?' asked Oona as they set off once again.

Dotty shook her head. 'Only squirrels and rabbits. Though his aim ain't what it used to be,' she replied with a smile.

'Why don't he set snares?'

'He did once.'

'Not anymore?' Oona looked at the woman questioningly.

'He found a rabbit in one, only it weren't dead. The sight of its suffering and the need to wring its neck did for him when it came to trapping the beasts,' she explained. 'There's one thing I'll say for his shooting; his first shot kills them dead more often than not.'

They fell into silence as the burble of the creek became louder. Its sparkling waters were glimpsed between the trunks and the ground became more uneven.

'We'll skirt along its course,' said Dorothy, noting the increasing difficulty of the girl's passage despite the improvement of the injury.

Walking upstream with the creek to their right, they fell into a comfortable silence. Oona began to swing their hands to and fro, a contented expression upon her youthful face.

''The spring, it brings new birth,' Oona said lyrically. 'The earth a song of joy, I sing in praise of You, for I'll be coming home.'

'What's that?' asked Dorothy.

'A song that Etty done taught me. She sung it me to help me sleep,' she replied. 'The summer, it brings the heat, the beat of the blazing sun, to ripen the harvest of the soul, for I'll be coming home.

'The fall, it brings the reaping, the weeping of tree and sky, soft farewells and fading light, for I'll be coming home.

'The winter, it brings the sleep, the deep snows that cover all, in the death that ain't truly so, for I'll be coming home to You, oh Lord, for I'll be coming home.'

Dorothy looked at her affectionately. 'It's beautiful. Thank you for sharing it with me,' she commented with a warm smile.

Oona beamed, gladdened by the compliment and their surroundings as they continued through the forest.

25

'You shouldn't have paid him anything,' said Fitch as they rode at a leisurely pace along the track, the shadows of pines falling across them from time to time. 'He would have let us take the whisky and feed without grumbling,' he added before drawing on the roll-up hanging from the corner of his mouth.

'Because you had your hand on your gun,' replied Wallace. 'I ain't no common thief.' He shot his partner a hard glance.

'You saying I am?' asked Fitch with an edge to his tone, smoke issuing forth with his words.

'Did you hear me say that? Did you even hear me say something remotely like that?' responded Wallace.

Fitch stared over at him, brow tight with annoyance. 'You sure are a moralising pain in the ass,' he stated.

'What, because I wouldn't take from an honest man?'

'And you know he's honest how?'

'That's not the point,' said Wallace.

'What is the point?'

'It don't matter a jot if he were honest, as long as we ain't stealing. There's right and wrong, and that's just plain wrong.'

'But killing niggers ain't?' retorted Fitch with a raised eyebrow, flicking the cigarette butt to the side.

Wallace turned to him. 'We're doing what we're employed to do and within the laws of this fair country. Besides, when did you give two hoots about killing niggers?'

'Never,' replied Fitch, 'but I thought maybe you was going soft on me.'

Wallace spied a figure coming around a bend in the track fifty yards away, the trees still partially hiding them. 'Looks like we've got company,' he said, aware that his companion was still looking at him and nodding forward.

Fitch turned to stare at the bearded and bedraggled man ahead. He was on foot, cooking utensils tied to his pack clanking as he walked. Their sounds marked his slowing pace as the distance closed and the stout bounty hunter rested his hand upon the handle of his gun.

Ethan moved to the side of the road and came to a standstill, measuring the two men with his gaze as they drew near. 'Spare any food or maybe a coin or two?' he called.

The bounty hunters brought their horses to a halt just before drawing level with the man's position.

'We'll give you coin in exchange for information,' said Wallace. 'We're looking for a nigger gal who goes by the name Oona Mae. She's lost property, so to speak. You seen or heard anything we might be interested in?'

Ethan pondered and shook his head. 'Can't say I have.'

'Nothing comes to mind?' asked Fitch.

'Nothing. Which way was she headed?'

'East.'

'There's settlers in the forest who may have seen something,' he offered, pointing off the track behind him.

The bounty hunters both glanced in the direction indicated.

'They live in a cottage that ain't much more than a shack and there's bird tables all about.'

'Much obliged,' said Wallace, reaching into his pocket.

'We ain't going to pay him for that,' stated Fitch. 'He ain't told us nothing about the nigger's whereabouts.'

'He still gave us information that might help,' replied Wallace as he took out a coin.

He placed it on his forefinger and flicked it towards the man with his thumb. A small puff of dust rose into the air where the coin landed on the side of the dirt track in front of Ethan, who quickly bent and picked it up.

'Much obliged,' he stated.

Wallace gave his horse a nudge in the flanks and turned it eastward. Moving off the track, he began to pass into the trees as Fitch remained in station, unhappy that his partner had paid the beggar.

'You coming?' asked Wallace over his shoulder.

Fitch glared at him and glanced at the man as he considered pulling his gun and demanding the payment back. With a snort and shake of his head, he kicked his horse and set off.

'Oh, and by the way,' called Ethan after them, Wallace looking back. 'Don't make the same mistake I did. They're husband and wife, not father and daughter.'

26

The land began to climb and their speed declined as Oona and Dorothy continued through the trees with the creek to their right. A spire of rock rose above the forest in the middle distance, bushes clinging to crevices and a hawk briefly circling above before flying towards higher peaks to the north. A waterfall came into view as they came over a rise, walls of rock embracing it to either side.

'Here we are,' announced Dorothy. 'This is the special place I wanted to show you. I call it Eden Falls.'

Oona looked through the thinning trees, enthralled by the natural splendour of the falls. The waters plunged to a wide pool of pale blue. A few trees peered over the edge of the cliff, as if measuring their courage to jump, the forest marching north and surrounding the spire of rock.

They walked out of the pines and onto a spit of land overlooking the pool. Oona's feet were brushed by lush grass as they walked to the edge and peered over, the water eight feet below.

'We call this "The Overlook",' said Dorothy, taking a couple of steps back and removing the leather bag from her shoulder.

'You want to help me spread the blanket?' she asked, pulling open the flap and taking out the patchwork within.

Oona walked over as Dotty unrolled it. They took hold of the corners and settled it on the grass.

'We'll take a dip and then eat. There's a little path that'll take us down to the water,' said Dorothy, nodding to the right of the outcrop. 'How does that sound?'

'Good,' replied Oona.

Dotty began to undress, neatly laying her clothes out on the blanket. The girl followed suit, the two of them soon standing naked in the sunshine.

'Come on.' She held out her hand.

Oona took hold after taking up her stick and they made their way to the vague track that wound down steps of rock beside the outcrop. They passed down, Dorothy taking the lead. Reaching the bottom, they stood on an earthy patch of bank, the pool rippling before them.

'It's deep enough to dive right in,' said Dotty, releasing the girl's hand and doing just that.

She splashed into the clear waters and Oona could see her take a couple of strokes beneath before resurfacing a few yards away. She shook her head, strands of hair loosing a cascade of glittering droplets into the air.

'Come join me,' she called with a wave of her hand.

'I can't swim,' she admitted, the thought of the deep water making her fearful. 'I've only done paddled and waded before.'

'Just jump in, I'll see to your safety,' encouraged Dorothy with a smile.

Oona looked at the cool blue waters. Her fear outweighed by her wish not to disappoint, she set the stick down and leapt from the bank. Closing her eyes, she dropped into the pool like a stone, an arcing spray of water marking her entry.

Once beneath the surface, she began to flail. A sense of panic quickly came upon her as she opened her eyes narrowly and looked to the light above, her body sinking from its presence.

A hand suddenly grasped her arm and she was heaved through the resistance of the water, feeling it push against her cheeks. Her head broke the surface and she took desperate breaths, blinking her vision clear.

'Paddle with your feet,' instructed Dorothy as she continued to retain a hold on the girl, seeing the look of fright upon her face.

Oona did as she was told, finding her shoulders lifting slightly from the water and gaining in confidence.

'That's it, keep going.'

Her ankle giving her a little pain, Oona kept herself afloat.

'Put your arms out to the sides and use your hands like oars to relieve the effort of your feet if needed,' said Dotty. 'Like this.' She released the girl and held station nearby, guiding by example as she gently moved her hands beneath the surface.

Oona followed her lead. She remained buoyed and began to enjoy the sensations of being immersed as the warmth of the sun rested upon her face and shoulders. She smiled, brightened by her success and relieved after her initial fear.

Dorothy cupped her hands and playfully splashed the girl. Oona looked at her in surprise, water running down her face. Seeing the woman's amused expression, she sent a shower of water back towards her, the pair of them laughing as the air was filled with droplets that captured the light of the spring sun.

Breathless and filled with forgetfulness, Oona felt the ache in her legs and shoulders as the game came to an end. 'Can we eat now?'

'That's just what I was going to suggest,' replied Dorothy, looking up at The Overlook. Her expression immediately became more sombre and Oona looked over her shoulder.

The native girls she'd seen by the stream stood above, hand in hand and as still as deer.

'It be them,' breathed Oona.

Dorothy turned to her with a curious look.

'I saw them in the forest when I were sitting by the stream,' she expanded, turning to the woman. 'Have you seen them before?'

'The Creek that remain in the forest come here to bathe from time to time,' she said with a nod.

'Do you know their names?' asked Oona excitedly.

'No. Since the days when the men came to trade, there ain't been a word exchanged between us and them. They keep themselves to themselves,' she answered. 'I'd best get out and make sure they aren't to taking our things.'

Dorothy swam to the bank and pulled herself out, the older sister stiffening and looking as if she were about to turn tail and run. Straightening, Dotty looked up at the girls. 'Food?' she enquired, holding an imaginary piece of bread between her fingers and putting it into her mouth.

The older girl turned and quickly began to walk away, her sister staying at her side. With a backward glance, she entered the forest and they soon vanished from sight, the trunks concealing their retreat.

Oona slowly moved towards the bank, remaining upright in the water. Reaching it, she climbed out and took up her stick, getting to her feet. 'Do you think they'll be coming back?'

'Not while we remain,' replied Dorothy as she made her way up the path beside The Overlook, Oona following after. 'There ain't many left now, but I've seen them a few times.'

'Here?'

'On occasion,' replied Dorothy.

'The same girls?'

'Questions, questions,' said Dotty in amusement as she reached The Overlook. 'You remind me of Ezra when he was your age. He never stopped asking them and I'll answer all yours once we've dressed and eaten. How's that sound?'

Oona nodded and looked off into the woodland, hoping to glimpse the natives one last time. Seeing no sign, she walked over to where her clothes rested on the blanket, Dorothy already dressing. Picking up her underwear, she followed suit, her stomach groaning and ready for food.

27

Walter carried the armchair out of the cottage and placed it on the grass before the porch. Glancing up at the gaping hole in the overhang, he slipped the Hessian sack from beneath his arm and placed it on the upholstery so that it wouldn't get muddied.

Bending, he opened a small brown paper bag resting on the edge of the porch and took out some nails. Placing them between his lips, he picked up his hammer and a handful of shingles from a small pile beside.

Stepping onto the chair, he balanced the shingles on the overhang, the topmost slipping and threatening to fall due to the gentle pitch of the roof. Hand ready to catch it, the shingle settled and he turned his attention to the hole.

The whinny of a horse drew his gaze to the south. His temporary excitement at the possibility of his son's arrival was quickly replaced by an expression of concern. Two men were approaching through the pines. One was walking ahead, a cigarette hanging from his mouth as he studied the ground. The other was taller and a few steps behind, leading a pair of horses as he focussed his attention on the cottage.

Spitting the nails onto his palm as he climbed down from the chair, Walter put them into the pocket of his corduroys. 'Good afternoon,' he greeted with a nod as the men entered the clearing with their horses a few steps behind.

'Good day,' replied the second man as the other flicked the cigarette he'd been smoking to the ground.

Walter's grip on the hammer tightened when he caught a glimpse of the pistol slung at the shorter man's hip. 'Can I help you gentlemen?' he enquired, disquieted by their approach.

They made no immediate reply, continuing towards him and coming to a halt a few yards shy.

'I'm John Wallace, this…' He held his hand towards his companion, '…is Felix Fitch.'

'Walter Brightwater,' he replied out of politeness.

Fitch moved towards the front door to the cottage.

'What's your business here?' asked Walter, glancing at Fitch and his agitation increasing.

'We're looking for lost property,' replied Wallace as Fitch stepped onto the porch and made to enter the house.

'Hey! This is private property,' said Walter, stepping around the chair.

Fitch turned to him and pulled his jacket back, the revolver in plain sight.

'He's only going to take a look about,' said Wallace, raising his hands disarmingly.

Walter turned back to the taller man. 'What property are you looking for?'

'A nigger gal,' replied Wallace. 'She ain't but thirteen and goes by the name Oona Mae,' he added, studying the old man closely.

There was a flicker of surprise and fear in Walter's expression which he tried to hide by looking to the ground as if in thought. 'Can't say I've seen the like. Don't get many visitors here and I ain't never seen a negro in the forest.'

Fitch moved to stand in the doorway and glanced about the interior. His gaze came to rest on the covers and pillow on the floor in the near right corner, the limited space between the chimney breast and front wall indicating that a child slept there.

'You got any children?' he asked over his shoulder.

'No, it's just me and my wife,' replied Walter nervously.

Fitch looked to his companion and gave a shallow nod.

'You sure you ain't seen her likeness?' asked Wallace, raising an eyebrow as he regarded him.

Walt nodded.

'This is a fine weapon,' commented Fitch, reaching inside and picking up the crossbow leaning by the door.

He turned to Walter. 'You know,' he began, 'you really shouldn't leave it loaded.'

Fitch pulled the trigger and the bolt flew. A scream of agony filled the clearing, birds disturbed from the trees and calling in alarm.

28

Oona watched as a large white butterfly settled on the grass beside the picnic blanket, its wings edged and veined with black. She sidled closer, staring at it and in awe of its simple beauty.

'That's a swallowtail,' stated Dorothy as she watched the girl reach out towards the insect, which took to the wing and flitted over the side of The Overlook.

Oona turned to her. 'Do you know all their names?'

'Some. My father taught me. We'd go for walks on a Sunday afternoon after church and he'd point them out.'

The girl glanced back to where the swallowtail had vanished from sight. Her stomach full and sitting in the sunshine surrounded by nature's glory, she felt content and at ease.

'What day is it today?' she asked, a thoughtful look upon her face.

Dorothy pondered a moment. 'It just so happens that it's Sunday,' she smiled.

'Don't you go to church anymore?'

'Of a sort,' she replied. 'This is where I give praise to the Lord; in nature.'

Oona looked at her in puzzlement. 'In nature?'

'Look around you,' she said, opening her arms. 'This place is a cathedral made by His own hand. What better place to be with God?'

'A cathedral?'

'A very big church,' explained Dorothy without a trace of condescension.

Oona looked around at the picturesque surroundings and nodded. 'I ain't never thought of it like that before.'

'Besides, there ain't a church closer than half a day's walk and Walt's legs ain't what they used to be,' she added with a wink.

Oona chuckled. 'How'd you meet?'

'My daddy hired him to help on the farm. I weren't but your age and Walter a good twenty years older, but boy was he handsome? And he could charm the hind legs off a donkey.'

'Your pa didn't mind?'

'He did, and then some. We'd meet in secret. I'd sneak out of the house in the middle of the night and he'd be waiting for me in one of the barns or in the orchard when summer came. When my daddy discovered what was happening, I was forbidden from mixing with the hands and Walt was dismissed.'

'What did you do?'

'Packed my things and went with him. I was hot headed and filled with vinegar. There weren't no one going to stop us being together. By hap of chance, Walt had inherited a haberdashery from his aunt and we set up shop together. I've always been good with a needle and created curtains and the like of my own design. They turned out to be quite the hit with well-to-do types and we thrived.'

Oona looked at her in puzzlement. 'What set you to moving out here?'

Dorothy sighed. 'We'd had enough of the city. We gave what we made from selling our belongings to the needy and looked to live as true Christians.'

'And your pa? What did he do?'

'I never saw him again after leaving with Walt,' replied Dotty, 'and he's long since dead.'

Oona regarded her a moment. 'You ever regret leaving?'

Dorothy smiled softly. 'Never,' she replied. 'I cherish every day with Walt. Even the six months we spent under canvas while building the cottage was an adventure.'

'I hope I'll be finding someone to love one day.'

Dorothy reached out and settled her hand upon the girl's shoulder. 'It may be you shall, but you will always have a relationship with God,' she said warmly. 'He loves you; provides you with food, water and the very air you breathe. All things come from Him and are therefore part of Him, so love the Lord in all His forms.

'Even squirrels?'

'Even squirrels,' laughed Dotty. 'Everything is sacred, so tend to this good Earth and only take what you need.'

'Etty would say similar,' nodded Oona.

'Then she was very wise,' said Dotty, winking again and squeezing the girl's shoulder.

Oona smiled and turned to the falls. The sound of the water washed over her as she turned her gaze heavenward. 'You think He judges us on heart or deed?' she asked, trying not to weigh the question too heavily.

'Deed,' answered Dorothy without hesitation. 'You can have the best intentions at heart, but it is your deeds that show your truth. This world is like a pond. Words can create ripples upon its surface, but actions create currents beneath.'

'What if you was driven to do something bad by the deeds of another?' She turned back to the woman, holding her gaze.

'Every word and every deed is a choice that you make. There ain't no other to blame.'

Oona's expression fell.

Dotty noted the change. 'What did you do?' she enquired softly.

The girl swallowed, fighting the urge to reveal what had happened, fearful of Dorothy's reaction and certain that no good would come of it. It was the darkest of secrets, one which carried a sickness that tainted her and was able to spread to others should they know what she'd done.

'Nothing,' replied Oona, shaking her head and looking into the forest.

'It don't seem to be nothing that you're struggling with,' she observed, 'but if you don't want to spill, I ain't going to force you to do so.'

She removed her hand from the girl's shoulder and began to wrap what little remained of the food. Oona looked at her, words catching in her throat as the internal battle continued to rage.

Unable to vocalise her sin, she reached for the cheese, wrapping the brown paper back around it. Taking up the accompanying piece of cord, she tied and handed it to Dorothy.

The woman took the small packet and looked into her eyes. 'Something haunts you, and I'll wager it's more than the mean spirited treatment that you've endured,' she stated. 'Let your past go, Oona. It is done and whatever your deeds, they belong to yesterday. Today you are a sweet girl, a precious child.'

Dorothy raised her free hand to the girl's cheek and stroked it with the backs of her fingers. 'Such a precious child.'

Oona withdrew from the contact and vigorously shook her head. 'I ain't what you think I am,' she stated, tears in her eyes.

'Yes, you are, only you cannot see it because of the shadow that follows you,' responded Dorothy with a sad smile.

'I…' Oona burst into tears and covered her face, unable to reveal what she'd done.

Dorothy put the packet down and moved forward, taking the girl into her arms and holding her tight.

Her tears slowly abated and she sniffed deeply, wiping her eyes as she looked up at the woman's face. 'I'm sorry,' she whispered.

'Ain't nothing to apologise for,' reassured Dorothy, stroking her back. 'Come on, we should pack up and be on our way,' she added. 'Walt is probably wondering where we've got to.'

She moved away from Oona and collected up the last of the food. 'What's the betting he ain't even got started on that roof yet?' she asked, looking over with a grin. 'A snail would get it done quicker.'

Oona couldn't help but smile in response, feeling lighter after shedding her tears and finding acceptance in Dotty's arms. She got to her feet without needing the aid of the stick and helped her fold the blanket, which was stuffed into the bag in readiness to leave.

Dorothy held out her hand and found it grasped with eagerness. She looked to Oona's profile, noting that the strain had vacated. Leading her from The Overlook, they went into the pines, following the course of the creek, the sounds of the waterfall receding.

'I don't think I be needing the stick anymore,' commented Oona, lifting it to show that she wasn't using it to walk.

'I'm glad you're making such a quick recovery. As you get older, the time you need to mend gets longer until one day there's no more mending to be had,' she said with a glance.

They continued on in silence, savouring the surroundings. Dorothy veered to the right and they moved away from the creek, passing deeper into the forest.

'How did you know when to turn for the cottage?' asked Oona.

'Did you notice the half-moon of rocks on this side of the creek?'

The girl nodded. 'That's where I were bathing yesterday.'

'When you reach them, it's time to make your way west.' She glanced at Oona thoughtfully. 'Are you still fixing on heading north sometime?'

She shrugged in response.

'You know you're welcome to stay. It's an awful long way to be trekking through this country and you're likely to run into some unsavoury types.'

'I done heard much talk about the free states,' replied Oona. 'Seems like they be where I should be heading.'

'But you're free here.'

'Only with you. I ain't heard of any other white folks treating negroes like you and Walt.'

'True,' conceded Dotty, 'but it only takes a couple to make all the difference,' she added with a smile, squeezing the girl's hand.

'You've done made a heap of difference, but the north still calls.'

'We'll be sad to see you go,' responded Dorothy.

The cottage could be glimpsed between the trunks and she looked to the armchair placed by the porch. A few shingles were scattered on the ground nearby, having slipped from the pile that rested on the edge of the roof.

She slowed her pace, brow becoming furrowed. 'Something ain't right,' she stated, noting the piece of sackcloth that lay on the ground beyond the chair, the breeze having lifted it from the seat.

'What?' asked Oona, keeping her voice lowered as she felt the woman's tension transmitted through the bond of their hands.

Dorothy went still as they reached the edge of the clearing.

'Dotty?' she looked up at the woman's worried expression.

'There's blood,' she whispered in response, seeing a dark spatter upon blades of grass near the armchair.

'Blood? Where?' Oona's pulse raced as Dorothy pointed.

'Stay here,' she instructed without taking her eyes from the cottage.

Releasing the girl's hand, she crept forward, noting that the window shutters had been closed, the door open on the bright day. 'Walt?' she called hesitantly.

There was no response.

'Walt, you in there?' she called again as she drew nearer.

Oona watched with wide eyes, body beginning to tremble and stomach churning.

Dorothy stepped onto the porch and went to the door. She suddenly came to a halt, body stiffening. 'Who are you and where's my husband?'

'He's taken to his bed,' replied a man's voice as Oona stepped to the nearest pine, concealing herself behind and peeking out, free hand to its trunk.

Dorothy turned from the two men leaning against the edge of the table opposite the door. Looking to the bed in the gloom of the far left corner, she saw Walter lying on the covers, but discerned no movement.

'Where's the nigger gal?' asked Fitch as he took up the crossbow from the table.

'I don't know what you're…'

He raised the weapon, pointing it towards her chest. Dorothy took a step back from the door, raising her hands.

Fitch glanced at the blankets and pillow by the chimney breast. 'Where is she?' he reiterated, finger tightening on the crossbow's trigger.

Dorothy stood a moment. Quickly turning, she stepped towards the edge of the porch, looking to where Oona hid in the tree line.

Her mouth fell open and she staggered to a stop, stepping heavily from the porch. Peering down in shock, she stared at the head of the bolt protruding from her chest.

Oona watched in horror, nails digging into the bark of the pine.

Face paling and teetering as she stood, Dorothy turned to Oona. 'Run,' she mouthed, eyes pleading with the girl to go as she fell to her knees and toppled forward onto the grass.

29

Oona dropped the walking stick and ran into the forest. Gritting her teeth against the pain in her ankle, she was overcome by panic.

The ground made a hollow sound beneath her bare feet as she made for the creek. She didn't dare look back, the image of Dorothy with the bolt projecting from her chest driving her onward.

Spying the waters through the trees, she headed upstream on the even ground, following its course northward. Finally braving a backward glance, she was relieved to see no sign of pursuit.

Eden falls came into view and she made for The Overlook. Moving out onto the thick grass, Oona came to a standstill upon the flattened area where the blanket had rested.

She fought for breath, throat thick with phlegm. Looking around, she tried to focus her thoughts. 'Where do I go?' she wheezed, scratching the side of her head.

The snap of a twig in the direction from which she'd come set her legs in motion. She moved to the side of The Overlook and made her way down the track to the bank. Without a second thought, she climbed into the water, not wishing to jump for fear the sound of her entry would alert her pursuers to her presence.

Slipping fully clothed into the water, she made her way across to the far side. Her progress was slow as she remained upright, bobbing like a cork as she paddled with her hands.

She pulled herself out with the help of a root and crawled on hands and knees, concealing herself in the thick undergrowth. Breathless and filled with tremors, she sat in the ferns and looked across at the far bank, raising her gaze to The Overlook and trees beyond.

The sun quickly dried any trace of her exit from the pool as she caught her breath. She wiped water from her eyes, its coolness helping in the calming of her agitated state. The trembling of her body subsided, the beating of her heart no longer felt in her throat.

Suddenly becoming motionless, she stared across as two men materialised out of the forest. One led the other, back bent as he scanned the ground for evidence of her passage, Walter's crossbow slung over his shoulder. Their guns were drawn, the second man scanning the surroundings with eyes narrowed and horses in tow.

They moved out onto The Overlook, the man at the front reaching the flattened grass and looking about. He toyed with something about his neck as he straightened, the other man coming to a standstill beside and looking at him questioningly.

'There's a lot of disturbance here,' stated Fitch, the tramplings of Oona and Dorothy's earlier visit disguising the girl's recent activity.

'You saying you don't know where she's gone?' asked Wallace.

'I'm saying, there's a lot of disturbance,' replied Fitch with irritation. 'You're welcome to do the tracking if you think you can do any better.'

'So, which way did she go?'

Fitch exhaled with exaggeration, glancing at the grass. 'This way,' he stated, leading them to the track at the side of The Overlook.

Oona watched with baited breath as they descended and moved to stand by the pool.

'Fancy a swim?' asked Wallace with brows raised as he looked at the water and then stared across at the far bank.

A shiver passed through her as his gaze lingered on the ferns in which she was concealed.

Fitch looked downstream. 'There's some rocks where we can cross,' he stated, nodding to indicate the boulders.

Wallace followed his gaze, looking at the proposed crossing before turning to his companion. 'You absolutely sure she's gone across? If she ain't, we'll be wasting a heap of time going over.'

Dropping to one knee, Fitch studied the bank, flicking a piece of debris aside with a finger. 'Two people went in and got out,' he stated eventually.

'She ain't over there, then?'

Fitch sighed. 'There ain't no way to tell for sure,' he admitted as he rose and looked across the pool.

'We should check there's no other tracks up there,' said Wallace, looking up at The Overlook. 'Could be she's gone north.'

'And if there ain't no other tracks?'

'We come back and take those rocks across.' He turned to Fitch. 'Don't fret, you'll be adding another tooth to that necklace of yours soon enough,' he stated, moving towards the track and heading back up.

Wallace reached The Overlook and stepped aside as he waited for Fitch to take the lead. His companion walked past him, going back to the area of flattened grass before widening his search for further tracks.

'Here,' he called, waving Wallace over without looking up.

Wallace joined him and studied the ground, unable to see anything of significance. 'What is it?'

'Another track. It heads northwest into the forest,' he stated.

'Is it the nigger gal's?'

'Looks that way. It's definitely a child, though there looks to be another with her.'

Wallace looked at his companion's profile in confusion. 'Two kids?'

Fitch shrugged. 'Maybe the nigger lovers had one of their own.'

Standing in thought a moment, Wallace took a breath. 'Well, it's the best lead we got, so we'd best follow it.

They moved steadily away from The Overlook, Fitch focussing his attention on the scant evidence of passage amidst the pine needles and rocks. Wallace remained a couple of steps behind, gun drawn and expectant of finding their prey as he led the horses through the trees.

30

She sat within the undergrowth for long minutes after the men had disappeared from view. Gathering her courage, Oona moved away from the creek, wincing at every whisper made by the fern fronds as they brushed against her clothing and skin.

Her heart beating apace and terrified that a call of discovery would arise at any moment, she got to her feet. Her ankle throbbed, but the pain was mild.

Hobbling through the trees, she was confronted with a rough cliff that loomed before her. It encircled the eastern bank and she could see no break or easier route.

Unwilling to retreat for fear of stumbling into the men, she began to ascend. A flurry of small stones was loosed by her hand, skittering and bouncing down the incline. She went still, drawing herself close to the cold rock.

Waiting a while, she heard only the waterfall. Hands gripping tight and bare feet finding purchase, Oona continued to make the climb.

Reaching the top, she moved away from the drop on her hands and knees, looking over her shoulder in relief. Getting to her feet, she set off through the trees, which grew sparser in the increasingly rocky terrain. Bushes became more prominent as she moved beyond the spire of rock she'd spied that morning, keeping the creek to her left as she headed north.

It wasn't long until the landscape became more mountainous and Oona stepped from one rock to another. The pines had thinned, their breeze-stirred whisperings no longer collective, but solitary. She glanced back regularly, nervous of pursuit, but seeing no evidence of such.

Passing around a spine of rock that brought to mind the bones of some gigantic beast, she set eyes on a wooded fold in the land. It was sheltered on three sides; a high slope rising to the rear and embracing it with rock-strewn arms.

She moved into the fold, in need of rest and hopeful that it would provide somewhere for her to recoup in hiding. Entering the trees, she moved through them with increasing difficulty, her ankle aggravated by the effort of her escape.

Spying tree stumps through the trunks ahead, she came to a stop. She looked about for further evidence of human activity, pulse becoming elevated once again. Her gaze settled on a dark mouth in the base of the slope a hundred yards ahead.

'A mine,' she stated, making out wooden props and a stone lintel above the entrance that was cracked and threatening to cave in.

Glancing back, she made her way out of the trees. Passing through the wasteland of stumps, she noted that they were blackened and rotting, fungi growing upon their sides and in dank crevices. Her wariness lessened with the realisation that the trees had long since been cut down and she approached the mine with greater haste, longing to be hidden from prying eyes.

Hovering at its dark entrance, she raised her hand to the lintel, finding it solid despite the sizeable crack. 'Hello?' she called tentatively, staring into the pitch black that swallowed the daylight fifteen yards into the mine.

The weak echo of her voice was the only reply.

Looking back towards the trees, she entered, a chill to the air as she moved beyond the entrance. Faint dripping accompanied her steps as she passed through a short passage and found the walls to either side falling away and out of sight in the darkness.

A creature scrambled from her approach, claws scraping on stone. Thinking it likely a rat, she peered into the depths, her eyesight adjusting, but only allowing her to see a little more of the space about her.

Moving to the left of the entrance passage, she bent and placed her hands to the ground. Finding it dry, she settled with her back to the wall, yawning as she did so. Gooseflesh arose on her arms in response to the cold and she wrapped them about herself, drawing her knees up in the hope of holding onto some of the heat of her body.

Weariness overtook her, lids slowly closing. She battled to remain wakeful, worried that the men may come upon her as she slept, head nodding down in small increments.

Lifting it quickly, Oona blinked and tried to rouse herself by rubbing her arms, hoping the activity would chase away her sleepiness. Leaning around the corner, she peered out of the mine, finding no sign of anyone in the wasteland or woods beyond.

'You'll be safe here,' she tried to reassure herself.

Withdrawing from the entrance's line of sight, she settled once more.

'Dotty,' she whispered, tears springing to her eyes as the sight of the woman pierced by the bolt replayed in her mind's eye.

Weeping, she bowed her head, feeling lost and alone. The sensations were greater than when she'd taken flight from the plantation, contrasted as they were with the brief happiness she'd found with the kindly couple.

Guilt weighed heavy upon her. It was her presence that had brought about the couple's demise. The shadow of her sin seemed inescapable.

She sniffed, the soft sound reverberating in the hollow of the mine. Slowly but surely, her tears subsided and sleep drew in, bringing with it a temporary relief from her condition.

31

Fitch came to a halt and Wallace drew up beside him with the reins in hand. They stared at the collection of huts amidst the trees ahead of them. A group of children sat in a circle about a large stone, banging nuts on its surface and casting off the shells. Placing them on a piece of blue cloth, they added the kernels to a wooden bowl already half full.

A woman sat before the cloth just outside the circle. She pierced the shells with a long needle, threading each onto a long cord.

'I think we've found who left the tracks,' said Wallace quietly.

'The nigger might be hiding in one of them shacks,' replied Fitch.

'You reckon Injuns would give shelter to anyone but their own?'

'I ain't to knowing an Injun's mind. Who knows what these savages think, if they think at all?'

'Ecke.' One of the youngest children pointed towards the men as she sat near the woman.

The circle of natives lifted their heads and peered through the trees. The woman putt down the needle and threaded shells. Getting to her feet, she began to walk towards the bounty hunters, skin dress hugging her lithe figure and long dark hair tumbling about her shoulders.

'What you want here?' she asked, coming to a stop.

'We're looking for a nigger gal,' stated Wallace, his left arm jolted back slightly as one of the horses bucked its head.

'No nigger girl,' responded the woman with a shake of her head.

'What about in the wigwams?' Fitch nodded towards the buildings.

'No nigger girl,' repeated the woman.

A man wearing a loincloth stepped out of the largest building at the centre of the small settlement. 'Cocheta?' he asked, noting the confrontation and walking over, his muscular body tanned and expression one of concern.

She turned to him and placed her hand upon his shoulder in a gesture of reassurance as he came to a stop.

'What they want, Cocheta?' he asked.

'Nigger girl.'

'We're looking for a nigger gal that's hiding out in this godforsaken forest,' said Fitch. 'You seen her?'

The man looked to him unkindly. 'Only Creek here.'

'Then you won't mind if we take a look for ourselves.' He began forward, but the man moved to block his way.

'Yaholo,' said Cocheta. 'Allow.' She glanced at the pistol upon Fitch's hip meaningfully.

He frowned and stepped aside reticently. 'You look, then go.'

Three more Creek men appeared from the far side of the buildings, spears in hand. Their expressions changed when they saw the bounty hunters and the tension in Yaholo's posture. They prowled towards them, as if hunting prey.

'We don't want any trouble,' said Wallace, raising his free hand submissively and glancing at his companion.

'But she could be inside,' complained Fitch, hand resting on his gun.

Wallace leant towards his companion. 'It ain't worth it,' he whispered. 'Let's go across the river. If there ain't no joy following that trail, we'll come back.'

'We're here now,' responded Fitch, the spears pointed towards him as the three huntsmen came to a halt beside Yaholo.

'So are they. You reckon you can take all of them before they put a hole in you that can't be plugged?'

'Both of us might.' Fitch looked at him pointedly.

'And both of us might not. I ain't being skewered for no nigger,' said Wallace.

'Go,' ordered Yaholo, pointing away.

Wallace took hold of his colleague's sleeve and gave it a tug. 'Let's be on our way.'

Fitch looked down at his hand in annoyance before turning his attention back to the Creek. 'I'll be seeing you,' he stated, his eyes narrowed and tone containing a threat.

Turning, he and Wallace set off back towards the waterfall, their horses plodding behind.

'Don't ever do that again,' growled Fitch.

'What? Save your life?'

Fitch shook his head and snorted. 'You've got one hell of an imagination.'

Wallace made no comment, continuing in the direction they'd come with his companion lagging behind. The Creek villagers watched, the men lowering their spears as the bounty hunters passed out of sight.

32

'She was hiding there all the time?' asked Wallace as he looked at the patch of disturbed ferns and Fitch straightened after examining the area.

'Looks that way,' he replied, peering into the woodland ahead, the waterfall at their backs. 'Probably watched us when we was on the far bank.'

'I'm looking forward to snagging this little bitch.'

'Do you think we should've asked for more now?' responded Fitch, raising an eyebrow as he turned to his companion.

Wallace gave him an irritated glance. 'I thought you'd agreed to drop the subject,' he said, looking back at their horses, which had been left on The Overlook. 'We going to leave them there?'

'I don't see any other option,' replied Fitch. 'She can't have gotten too far and they've got plenty of grass to eat.'

'What about the Injuns? I ain't of a mind to come back and find them stolen.'

'Fine. You stay here, I'll get the girl,' said Fitch as he set off into the trees. 'Only, I'll be wanting more than a fifty cut,' he added over his shoulder.

Wallace glanced back at the horses again and sighed. Setting off after his partner, he quickened his pace until he was only a step behind.

'So, money is important then?' said Fitch pointedly.

'Stop riding me about the goddamn money and track this nigger. The sooner we get this job done, the sooner we can move on.'

'It may be we should move on in different directions,' mumbled Fitch.

'That would be just fine by me,' responded Wallace.

They continued between the trunks in silence, both brooding and filled with irritation at the other's presence. A branch snapped under Wallace's boots and Fitch glared at him.

'You want to let the whole forest know where we are?' he said angrily as the cliff came into view through the trees.

'It ain't me who's talking loud enough to be heard back in Macon,' retorted Wallace.

Fitch came to a halt and turned to his companion, jaw clenching. 'What did you say?' he hissed.

'You heard me.'

'Say it again.' His hand went to the handle of his pistol

'You going to shoot me now?' Wallace looked at him incredulously. 'That don't seem like a wise move for someone so worried about noise,' he scoffed.

Fitch pulled his gun in one fluid movement and pointed it at Wallace's chest, drawing back the hammer with his thumb. 'Go on, say something else clever,' he challenged.

Wallace glanced at the barrel, arms remaining loose at his sides. 'What? You going to shoot me for talking?'

'I've shot people for less.'

'My brothers ain't going to be none too happy if you put a bullet in me.'

'I ain't scared of your brothers,' said Fitch.

'They're wanted for murder in three states.'

'You say.'

'You've seen the handbills,' replied Wallace.

Fitch continued to glare at him, the gun unwavering. He considered his course of action and eventually lowered the weapon. 'I'm going on alone.'

'You ain't getting more than a fifty cut,' stated Wallace.

'Fifty be just fine if I don't have to put up with your horse shit.' He turned away and walked up to the cliff. 'Go take care of the nags. I'll be back with the girl and I'll be wanting my share.'

'And that's all you'll get.'

Fitch ignored the response, holstering his pistol and beginning the climb. 'Should never have partnered up with the son of a bitch,' he grumbled.

'Who else'd put up with you when you're all cranky and bent out of shape?' responded Wallace as he watched.

'Who bends me out of shape in the first place?' countered Fitch as he reached the top and pulled himself over.

'Ornery bastard,' stated Wallace after his companion had vanished from sight. He turned and began back in the direction of the creek, thankful that they'd parted company.

Fitch moved away from the drop without a backward glance. He came to a halt by a tree and leant against its trunk, pulling his tobacco from his jacket and rolling a cigarette. Lighting it, he took a long drag and exhaled deeply, absently toying with the necklace of teeth. Beginning to unwind, he looked to the ground and began to follow the evidence of the girl's passage, moving through the thinning trees in virtual silence as he sought out his prey.

33

A man in his late twenties approached the cottage upon a ponderous horse. The brim of his grey hat was wide and drooping, shading his brown eyes. The shadow of stubble darkened his face, his features strong despite a little excess weight.

Ducking beneath a branch, he held the reins in one hand, the other resting upon his lap. He was enjoying the leisurely ride and in no hurry to endure his parents' questions and the fussing of his mother. Ezra knew both were conducted out of love, but they made his visits more vexing than relaxing.

Spying the cottage through the trunks, he halted the horse in order to take a moment to collect his thoughts, adjusting the collar of the pale shirt beneath his tan jacket. The announcement of Johanna's fifth child would be taken with great excitement, as would his promotion.

Ezra smiled as he pictured his mother's expression at both pieces of news. His father was always more sedate, a pat on the back sufficing on such occasions, but he knew that he was proud of him.

Nudging his steed in the flanks, he set off towards the humble dwelling. The horse plodded slowly, hooves heavy upon the mat of needles.

His mouth fell open when he saw the body lying in the grass before the porch. 'Ma?' he whispered, his expression filled with horror.

Leaping down, he sprinted through the last of the trees and into the clearing. Passing a couple of the bird tables, he came to an abrupt halt a short distance from the body.

Ezra looked breathlessly upon his mother, pulse racing. She was lying face down in the grass, crossbow bolt embedded between her shoulder blades. There was no trace of life other than the flies that fussed about the bloody wound.

He looked around. Seeing no sign of his father, he stepped around his mother's body and went to the porch. Going to the open door, he peered into the cottage and saw the figure lying on the bed in the far corner.

Hurrying across the room, his boots marked his fearful advance. He drew up beside the bed and looked upon the pale face and sightless eyes that greeted him. 'Pa,' he breathed.

He swallowed hard as he stared at the dried blood matting his father's beard and about his lips. A crossbow bolt rose from his torso, having pierced his lungs and caused him to choke on his own existence.

'What happened here?' he asked the corpse, shaking his head.

Tears welled in Ezra's eyes as he stood in shock and confusion. Perspiration glistened upon his face, his heart continuing to beat an agitated rhythm.

He turned to scan the interior. Whoever had killed his father had dragged his body in from outside, the back of Walter's boots having left scuff marks on the boards.

'Why kill them?' He shook his head again. His parents lived a peaceful life that did no harm and took no more than was needed. He could see no reason why anyone would take their lives.

'The gold!' he exclaimed in sudden revelation.

Pacing the length of the room, he went to the chimney breast. Examining the left side, he found what he was looking for. Prying out a loose stone with his fingers, he bent and set it upon the floor.

Ezra reached into the shadowy hole that had been revealed and took out a tin box. Opening the lid, he found a dark velvet pouch, a small pistol and a scattering of bullets within.

He crouched and placed the box beside the stone on the boards. Taking out the pouch, he opened the drawstrings and tipped it over his waiting palm. A small pile of gold nuggets spilled out, most no larger than apple seeds. All had been found during his father's years of panhandling and they gleamed even in the gloom of the cottage.

Ezra's brow creased as he looked at the gold in confusion. 'It wasn't a robbery,' he stated.

'Maybe Pa wouldn't give up its hiding place?' he glanced at his father's body.

'No, he wouldn't have risked their lives for the gold.'

He carefully tipped the gold back into the pouch and secured the top. Crouching, he placed it back in the box and lowered the lid, closing its simple fastening.

Ezra tucked the tin under his arm and began to straighten, suddenly going still. He stared at the pillow and blankets in the corner, furrows on his forehead deepening.

Stepping over, he examined them, perplexed as to their reason for being on the floor. The indent in the pillow suggested that someone had been sleeping there, but the limited space made it unlikely that either of his parents had taken to the basic bed, though he could think of no reason why they should do so in the first place.

'Maybe a vagabond came a wandering and they put them up,' he puzzled.

Unable to arrive at any satisfactory answer, he turned and walked to the table, setting the tin down. He breathed deeply and looked out of the door at his mother's body.

'I must bury them,' he stated, eyes glistening as he thought about the good news he'd expected to be telling them and their anticipated reactions.

With tears beginning to roll down his cheeks, he went to the bed. Rolling his father's body in the patchwork of fur, he pulled the bed cover from beneath and walked to the front door, pausing in the sunlight on the porch before stepping out to cover his mother's still form with the shroud.

34

He wiped his brow with the back of his hand as he leant on the spade at the foot of the second grave. Fresh mounds of earth marked the final resting places of his parents at the north edge of the clearing behind the house.

Ezra glanced at the roots he'd had to clear, laying in a heap nearby and bringing to mind severed limbs. His frown deepened as the long shadows of the forest ushered in the chill of evening.

Bending, he picked up four lengths of foraged wood that he intended to make into markers for the graves. Putting them under his arm and carrying the spade in his other hand, he made his way to the cottage and passed around the west side, looking at the bird tables that he passed and seeing that there was little seed left.

Going to the porch, he leant the spade by the open front door and took the lengths of wood inside. Ezra put them on the table, glancing at the tin that still remained in plain sight before stepping to the side in order to open the cabinet.

He took out the bag of seed and went back outside, moving to the first of the tables and pouring a little out. His father had tended the tables dutifully and he'd honour his memory by making sure they were furnished with food until his departure the following day.

Moving to a table at the edge of the clearing, he poured again. Some of the seed spilled to the ground and he looked down. Turning his head slightly when he noted something at the periphery of his vision, his gaze settled on a pale cigarette butt resting upon a fern frond.

He stepped over to it and set the bag of seed down. Picking up the butt, he briefly studied it. Gaze turning to the ground, he saw hoof prints nearby and discerned the vague impressions of boots.

'Two horses and two men,' he murmured, noting the direction of travel.

Ezra smelled the tip of the stub. 'Not too long ago.'

Rising and dropping the butt as he did so, he followed the tracks towards the cottage, the seed bag forgotten. Reaching the indent in the grass where his mother's body had lain, he glanced at the blood-darkened blades before seeking out further tracks.

He quickly spied what he was looking for and began towards the forest. Coming to a standstill at the tree line, he looked east through the trunks. 'The creek,' he stated to himself as thickening bands of cloud glowed orange and red in the sky above.

Ezra glanced up. 'The light will soon be gone,' he stated. 'I'll follow tomorrow.'

He turned and went back to the cottage, ignoring the blood stains but feeling their presence keenly. Entering, he shut the door without turning to the view, which was coloured by the sunset. Going over to the fireplace, the window shutters bumping against the frame as the wind began to strengthen, he took a couple of logs from the woodpile and added them to the flames already writhing in the grate.

Turning to the evidence of an unknown guest, he went to the covers. Lifting the edge of the topmost, he sniffed at it, finding only the musty scent that inhabited the cottage.

He folded it and followed suit with the second blanket, which looked to have been used to soften the hardness of the boards. The pillow tumbled from it and he picked it up once the task was done.

'Mother's handiwork,' he said, looking at the fresh stitching as he turned the pillow in his hands.

His brow furrowed when he noted a difference along one side. 'Except this,' he observed, the stitching rougher and indicating a less skilled hand.

He stared at it for long moments, puzzling over its meaning. Getting up with a wince, one of his knees clicking, he moved to the armchair before the hearth, carrying the pillow with him.

Sitting, he set it upon his lap and continued to try and unriddle the mysteries that surrounded his parents' demise. He could not fathom who had been sleeping upon the floor, nor who had worked on the pillow with his mother. He pondered over who'd approached the cottage and could arrive at no conclusion, frustration consuming him.

Ezra turned his gaze to the flames and their light played across his distressed features, their likeness captured in the sparkle of his tears. He began to weep, pillow gripped tightly upon his lap as he sat alone, darkness at his back.

35

Oona awoke in a womb of pitch black. The only evidence of the world's existence was the pain of rock digging into her side and the chill air upon her skin.

She shivered and pushed herself up, rubbing at her ribs through the dishevelled pinafore and housedress. It took a few moments to orient herself, the pressure of the darkness intensifying as the vivid memory of what had happened at the cottage came back to her.

Longing for light, she turned and put her hand to the rock face. Briefly following it on her hands and knees, she came upon the entrance passage and saw the soft light of the moon.

Oona got to her feet and made her way out of the abandoned mine, passing beneath the cracked lintel and coming to a halt. She raised her gaze to the heavens and stared at the clouds, which looked like the scales of a fish made luminescent by the moon beyond.

Taking deep breaths that were ushered away by the breeze, she calmed herself, hearing a wild beast bark in the woodland gathered in the fold of land before her. Her pulse returning to normal, she moved to the nearest tree stump, seating herself and yawning. She wiped away a tear and caught the scent of rotting wood and earth.

She scratched her wrists. Looking down at the scars, she found them ghostly in the light; the past haunting the present.

Etty came to mind as she recalled the old slave cleaning the cuts left by the manacles. She'd done so with tenderness, gently holding Oona's hands in turn and wiping away the blood with a cloth she wetted in a bucket. On the most recent occasion, they'd sat on the edge of the bunkhouse porch in the light of the full moon. They had been wordless, the actions serving to heal more than any amount of conversation.

'I miss you,' she whispered to the night.

A mouse scampered away from the far side of the stump, its foraging of fungi disturbed by her voice. She turned to the patter of its retreat, watching its dark shape vanish into the rocks.

She ran her fingers over the top of the stump, able to see the vague rings as she felt the ridges where the saw had once bitten. She imagined the pine standing tall, acting as a provider of food and shelter for the creatures of the wild.

Sliding from the top, Oona settled against the remains. 'We both been brought low without our consent,' she said softly, placing a palm to the bark. 'You was rooted in the ground, me in a life of slavery, but those lives be over now.'

She yawned and sighed. 'Those lives be over now,' she repeated, closing her eyes and putting her hands upon her lap beneath the pinafore.

36

Fitch woke with a snort. He sat beneath an overhang of rock, dark jacket buttoned up and collar raised. He released the revolver he'd been holding on his lap while sleeping, and flexed his fingers in order to renew the circulation.

'Should've got the bedroll from the horse,' he grumbled as he got up, keeping his head low.

Picking up the crossbow and quiver, he slung them over his shoulder and stepped clear of the overhang. Thick cloud had gathered during the night and the smell of rain was on the wind.

Moving off in the hope of picking up the slave girl's trail before it was washed away, he searched for clues as to her travels, the rocky landscape hampering his progress.

Fitch came to a halt and crouched, toying with his necklace as he examined the ground. A stone had been shifted out of place, the indent of where it had once rested visible beside. He looked around for further evidence of a trail, spying another disturbed rock a few yards away.

Taking his time, he followed the scant signs of passage towards a wood nestled in a fold in the landscape. Entering the trees, he moved through them in the dawn gloom. His gaze remained fixed upon the ground, a few scuff marks on bare patches of earth keeping him moving through the pines.

Tree stumps became visible ahead; mere silhouettes in the dim light. He broke from the woodland and paused, narrowing his eyes as he stared beyond the wasteland.

'An old mine,' he mumbled, taking the crossbow and quiver from his back.

Fitch put his foot on the stirrup at the end of the weapon and pulled the string back until the latch took hold. Taking a bolt from the quiver, he slipped it into the contraption and held it at the ready.

Finger to the trigger, he checked the ground and set off once again.

37

Oona opened her eyes to the greyness. The smell of the stump at her back was woven with damp earthiness that she found comforting as she sat in waking silence.

Clasping her hands together, she stretched her arms out before her as she yawned. Birdsong lifted from the woodland and she turned to her left to look at the dark trees.

She went still, eyes widening in dread. Someone was moving through the wasteland towards the mine. Their dark form was set against the backdrop of the woods as they crept between the trunks, but their presence was without doubt.

Oona began to tremble as the figure drew steadily closer and gained definition. She recognised the bearded and shadowy face as belonging to one of the men who had searched for her at The Overlook. She noted the weapon in his hands and realisation dawned; he was the man who'd killed Dorothy.

She held her breath as he came within ten yards of her position. She tried to remain still, arms clamped about her body in an attempt to control her quaking. His eyes were hidden in pools of darkness, but she was certain that his gaze was focussed on the entrance to the mine and she hoped he would pass without detecting her.

Fitch moved stealthily between the stumps, hunched and finger to the trigger of the crossbow. Following an old track made by whoever had once dug for gold in the mine, he barely blinked as he stared at the entrance.

Passing the last of the tree stumps, he hurried across the open ground without a sound, moving to the right of the entrance. Back to the rock, he waited a moment, listening for signs of occupation.

Ducking beneath the lintel, he slipped into the blackness.

Oona watched him disappear from sight. She inhaled deeply to relieve the strain on her lungs as she began to breathe once again, covering her mouth to mask the soft sounds.

She knew she had to escape while she had the chance, but found herself frozen in place by the idea that he was surveying the landscape from within the darkness. She chastised herself for such thoughts, sure the man would be moving deeper into the mine as he searched.

'Move,' she hissed as she stared at the entrance.

Oona forced herself to her feet and set off. She veered to the left, hoping to move beyond the man's sight should he peer from the entrance. She padded across the earth and stones, legs feeling hollow under the effect of her fear, which masked the aching of her ankle.

Nearing the woodland, she suddenly fell still. 'The other man?' she whispered.

Throat constricted, she stared into the trees. She could see no sign of the second man.

Looking back at the mine entrance, she felt trapped between its darkness and that which lurked beneath the boughs. Her imagination populated both with threat and kept her in place.

'You've only done seen one, and he be behind you,' she stated quietly.

Oona walked into the woodland, body coiled and stomach churning. She looked about, eyes like saucers and picking up a branch which she held like a weapon.

She was given a start as a bird fluttered in the trees, abruptly coming to a halt. Looking up, she saw a crow take to the wing and took a deep breath. Placing a palm to her breast, the violent beat of her heart was barely contained within her ribcage.

Turning, Oona looked back. Her nausea was redoubled, legs going weak as she spied the man coming across the wasteland.

She set off without hesitation, running despite the thought that the second man still lay somewhere ahead. Knowing that her pursuer must have followed her tracks, she tried to stick to stony ground.

The rain came as she exited the woodland, released in a curtain of grey that added to the gloom of the day. It was buffeted against the side of her face by the blustery wind as she moved beyond the protection of the fold in the landscape.

She went southwest, making her way towards the waterfall. She prayed the rain would mask her tracks and that the man who hunted her wouldn't expect her to go back.

The density of trees and bushes grew as she continued to run, throat thick and ankle throbbing slightly. Seeing the spire of rock that had been visible from the forest below the fall, she ran towards it, her fear that the second man was lying in wait driving her off her intended course.

Oona pushed through a thick growth of shrubs, thorns catching on her clothing and cutting her arms. Skirting the wide base of the spire, she made for the thick forest marching down the westerly slope. She entered the shadows, large droplets falling all about as the rain continued to pour.

Ducking beneath a branch, her pace was dramatically reduced by the tightly packed trunks. She wove between them, glancing back towards the spire, but seeing no sign of the man. The cuts on her arms stung, rainwater diluting the blood that seeped from them as she tried to block out the complaints of her body.

She heard the passage of water ahead, its source hidden from sight. With teeth gritted, she struggled onward, having to use nearby trunks to assist her passage.

38

Ezra walked out of the cottage and went to his horse, which was secured to the nearest bird table. It had taken a long time for him to find rest in the chair, unwilling to take to his parents' bed. He'd mourned his loss, shedding tears as the fire died in the hearth. The sleep that followed had been troubled and intermittent.

Going to the bulging saddlebags, he stared at them awhile, each containing food that had been intended to stock his parents' cabinet. Sighing, he rubbed the horse's neck and reached for the reins, slipping them from around the post.

Ezra began to lead the beast away, following the tracks left by the two men and their horses. Adjusting his hat, he glanced up at the cloudy sky. The rain had woken him, but had since passed, though the darkness drawing in from the north promised more.

He patted the pocket of his jacket as he reached the edge of the clearing, feeling the presence of the small handgun that he'd taken from the tin. Pausing, he looked back at the cottage. His gaze moved to the rear of the property, settling upon the graves and wooden crosses he'd placed at their heads upon waking.

'Goodbye,' he said softly, turning to the way ahead and walking into the pines.

He passed through the forest, intent upon the ground before him as heavy drops of rainwater continued to fall from the branches and pat against the needles. The hoof prints left the previous day were easy to follow, the earth indented and the trail clear.

Spying the creek between the trunks, Ezra found that the prints turned northward. Following their lead, he kept a wary eye on the woodland ahead as the ground began to rise slightly. He had no idea how far the men may have travelled and became more alert to their presence.

The whinny of a horse drifted through to him with the sounds of the creek.

Ezra went still, peering through the trees as his steed halted behind him and lowered its head, tugging at a clump of grass. 'The Overlook,' he whispered, looking at the grassy plateaux that reached from the trees, the waterfall beyond. Two horses grazed there, seemingly without supervision.

Releasing the reins and moving ahead in order to gain a better view, he spied a man seated against one of the trees at the edge of The Overlook. His hat was leant forward, covering his eyes as he apparently slept.

Ezra slid his hand into his pocket and took hold of the pistol. His grip made tight by anxiety, he crept forward.

He drew the gun as he neared the stranger's location, trying to control his breathing as his pulse raced. Lowering his stance, he approached the tree on cat's paws, seeing the man's shoulders to either side of the trunk and hearing a gentle snore.

Reaching the pine, he moved around to the right and aimed the gun at the man's head, cocking the hammer. 'Wake up,' he stated.

The man visibly jumped. He quickly shifted his hat onto his head with one hand as the other moved to his holster, going still when he set eyes on Ezra.

'Who the hell are you?' he asked, swallowing back.

'I'll be the one asking the questions,' replied Ezra. 'Move your hand away from the gun.'

Wallace looked at the barrel pointed at him. Hesitating a moment, he then withdrew his right hand and raised it in submission.

'Your name?'

'Wallace.'

'What are you doing here?'

'Looking for a runaway.'

Ezra's brow creased. 'A runaway?'

'A nigger gal. She's somewhere hereabouts.' Wallace lowered his hand to his lap.

'Yet you were sleeping.'

'My partner's on her trail. He'll be back anytime now.'

Ezra glanced to his right, looking at the two horses on The Overlook.

Wallace grabbed the barrel of his gun and the two men began to wrestle for control of the weapon.

The crack of a gunshot reverberated about The Overlook and waterfall. The horses leapt and bolted, galloping into the forest in fright.

Wallace's hands slipped from the pistol and he slumped sideways. Ezra stared in horror at the bullet hole in the man's cheek. The acrid smell of gun smoke caught in his nostrils as he straightened and staggered back, the pounding of hooves fading away.

'Shit!' His body trembled in the aftermath as a tear of blood ran down Wallace's face from the bullet wound.

Ezra calmed himself with deep breaths as he tried to think of what he should do. Looking to the edge of The Overlook, he moved to where Wallace lay dead, tucking the pistol into his pocket.

Taking hold of the dead man's hands, Ezra dragged him over the grass, keeping his gaze averted from the gory exit wound at the side of the bounty hunter's head. Wallace's Stetson came loose and was left in his wake, the wind taking and tumbling it to the side of The Overlook.

Ezra drew up beside the drop. Lifting the body by the armpits, he readied himself and threw it over the side with a grunt of effort.

Wallace's corpse fell like a stone, vanishing beneath the splash of its entry. Ezra peered over, seeing the stain of blood in the cool blue waters as the current took hold and slowly drew the body out of the pool, its velocity increasing as it was ushered downstream.

Stepping back, he looked to the far bank and the bluffs above the fall. Seeing no sign of the man's partner, he turned and fetched up the fallen hat, tossing it wildly over the southern edge of The Overlook.

Ezra considered what he should do, still none the wiser in relation to the fate of his parents. 'Maybe I should wait for his partner to return,' he pondered, glancing at the forest over his shoulder. 'Maybe the horses hold some clue.'

Turning, he stalked towards the trees, hands still shaking after the brutal turn of events. Reaching the pines, sudden nausea caused him to double over and vomit into the thick grass at the base of a nearby tree.

He gripped his stomach as he wretched, bile stinging his mouth. Spitting, he blinked tears from his eyes and breathed deeply to alleviate his condition.

Recovered enough to proceed, he passed into the woodland, the scent of pine helping to reduce his sickness further. 'I'll return for the horse,' he said to himself, glancing to where it waited in the trees as he began to follow the fresh hoof prints, thankful that the other steeds had stayed together in their flight and trying to concentrate on the task at hand so as not to think about what had happened.

39

Oona came upon the creek, both banks a few feet above the flow and crowned with rocks and pines. Breathless and weak, she held onto the trunk beside her for support as she looked up and down its course. A fallen tree joined the banks twenty yards upstream, the water frothing against rocks beneath as it rushed around a narrow bend from the east.

She made her way towards the crossing, every step taking great effort. Reaching the root bowl, she saw that it had ripped from the ground after some of the rocks and earth had collapsed into the flow.

Scrambling over the bowl, the roots slick, she got onto her hands and knees and began to make her way across the glistening trunk. Her strength waning, she found her arms and shoulders trembling with the effort, the branch that she was still carrying impeding her grip on the bark.

Her right hand slipped on moss and the branch was released in fright. Chest to the trunk and arms wrapping about it, she watched as the makeshift weapon was lost to the current, passing around a boulder and vanishing downstream.

Taking a moment to compose herself, she regained a secure hold and pushed her torso up. Muscles straining, Oona took greater care, each move measured as she made sure her grip was firm.

Nearing the far bank, she had need to pass around a branch that rose directly before her. She drew herself up to it, resting upon her shins. Taking hold, she began to sidle past.

There was a snap of breaking wood. Oona tumbled back, the broken branch still in her grip as she plummeted to the raging waters.

Splashing into the creek, her knee cracked on a blunt rock and she let out a yell of pain. She struggled to keep her head above the surface, thrashing desperately. Her vision was distorted, water running down her throat as she gasped for air.

She tried to kick. Agony filled her right knee and tears were forced from her eyes, only to be washed away in an instant.

The current took hold, dragging her down. Oona vanished from sight amidst the froth and rocks.

She fought without success. The creek had her in its grasp; turning and rolling her, buffeting her, sending her careening into boulders that bruised and battered. It took Oona under until her lungs were fit to burst, head breaking the surface and mouth opening in desperate need.

Her ears were filled with water that distorted the sounds about her. Her vision was blurred and face awash. Pain arose from numerous injuries and her body ached with exhaustion.

The fall came unexpectedly. Air and water mingled as she tumbled from on high; a rag doll amidst the waterfall's cascade.

40

Fitch arrived at the fallen tree. He looked along its length, noting scrapes and marks that indicated the girl had made her way across. His gaze fell on the stump of a broken branch near the other end and then moved to the forest on the far bank.

'I'm coming for you,' he mumbled, grabbing hold of roots and pulling himself up to the trunk, the crossbow having been returned to his back.

Fitch tested his weight, the tree unmoving. He began across, taking sidesteps. His boots threatened to slip on a couple of occasions and each time he paused to retain his balance.

Reaching the far side, he jumped down between a couple of branches. Looking to the ground, he sought signs of the girl's direction of travel. His brow creased as he passed around the top of the tree, scanning the bank but finding no trace of where she had disembarked from the fallen pine.

Widening his search, he still found no evidence. He stopped and stared back at the trunk, fondling his necklace as he pondered.

Fitch went back to the tree and leant out to the broken branch. Rubbing his thumb over the stump, he noted the scuff marks beside, but saw none any nearer.

Realisation dawned and he straightened. 'She fell in,' he stated, looking downstream.

'I ain't never known a nigger that can swim. Maybe the creek's done for her,' he said with a grin, taking out his tobacco and rolling a cigarette.

Licking the paper down after putting the pouch back into the inside pocket of his jacket, he retrieved a match.

He tried lighting it with his thumbnail, but the head came off and fell to the ground.

'Damp,' he said, smile fading.

Finding another match, he tried again, his action meeting with the same lack of success. Two more failures followed, the sulphurous tips coming away from the wood.

'Damn it!' Fitch tore the cigarette in two and threw the pieces to the ground in frustration.

A deep frown having replaced his grin, he headed downstream on the western bank of the creek. He scanned the water and rocks, hoping to see a bobbing corpse, but finding only splashing and froth. Regularly pausing, he looked to the far side and the ground before his feet, checking for any sign that she had managed to escape the flow.

41

They knelt upon the bank, a basket of dirty linens and clothes between. The older girl dunked the skin dress she was holding into the water as her sister struggled to wring out a blue cloth in her small hands. Lifting it onto her bare knees, she took the soap that was lying by the basket and rubbed it over the clothing.

There was a loud splash and they both looked up in alarm, staring at the pool beneath the waterfall.

The younger girl let out an exclamation and pointed to a figure visible beneath the disturbance of the surface, blue cloth hanging limp from her other hand.

They stared at the girl in the depths. She barely moved, arms and legs out to the sides as she remained deep in the embrace of the waters.

The older sister quickly put the soap and dress aside. Getting to her feet, she plunged in, swimming with strength to the location of the stranger.

Taking a breath, she dived under. Drawing herself to the girl with wide arcs of her arms, she took hold of her hand and pulled her to the surface.

Oona felt air on her face. Coughing and spluttering, she fought to clear her lungs and take in air.

'I have you,' reassured her rescuer, holding Oona against her and using one arm to take them towards the bank where her sister stood and waited.

Reaching out, she grasped a rock and pulled her ward alongside her. She said a few native words to her sister, who crouched and hesitantly took hold of Oona's shoulder to keep her in place.

The older girl climbed out, the tassels along the hem of her skin dress dripping as the moved to crouch beside her sister. Together and with great effort, they dragged Oona from the creek, moans of pain issuing forth.

Resting her on the grass and earth, they sat to either side and stared down at the unexpected arrival. Oona looked up at them, eyes reddened and blinking away blurriness.

'Talissa,' said the older girl, placing a hand to her chest. 'Mausi,' she added, indicating her sister with a nod.

'Oona,' she managed in response, coughing again and body convulsing, face contorting as her injuries made their presence known.

'You are hurt,' said Talissa. 'We fetch Ecke.'

'Ecke?' Oona's brow creased with a lack of understanding.

Talissa thought for a moment. 'Mother.'

She made to stand, but Oona reached out and weakly grasped her wrist. 'Don't leave.'

'We must have help. You cannot…' She pondered. 'You cannot walk this way,' she finished, surveying Oona's bruised and broken body.

'He be coming after me.'

Mausi looked across at her sister worriedly and briefly spoke in their tongue. Talissa frowned and looked to the top of the waterfall.

'Men hunt you?' she asked.

Oona nodded, wincing with pain.

'We see them. They come to us and ask of you. Erke… Father no want trouble.'

'Please, don't leave me here,' pleaded Oona, her grip becoming tighter and expression filled with fear.

Talissa looked to her sister and then glanced around. 'We hide you in rocks,' she stated.

Speaking to her sister and gently prying Oona's fingers from her arm, she got to her feet. Talissa and

Mausi took hold of her shoulders and began to pull her towards large boulders a little downstream.

Reaching the edge of the earthy patch of bank beside The Overlook, the sister's managed to get Oona into a sitting position, groans of discomfort issuing from her lips.

Talissa put her arm about her ward. 'You try stand,' she instructed.

Oona cried out as she put every effort into rising. Her right knee seared with pain and she nearly collapsed, the older sister only just keeping her on her feet.

She was guided into the boulders, placing her hands to them in order to remain upright and hobbling as best she could. Tears rolled down her cheeks as Talissa aided her passage, the native's face filled with tension. Mausi watched, remaining at the edge of the rocks and nervously glancing around from time to time.

'You hide there.' Talissa pointed at a deep cleft between two large rocks. The forest began a few yards to the right, overhanging branches adding to the concealment.

They moved towards the hiding place. Oona slipped and began to topple back. Talissa quickly adjusted her footing, placing her left on the sloping face of a rock. Bracing herself, she kept them standing, body trembling with exertion.

Clambering over the last boulders, they slipped down into the cleft, Talissa glancing curiously at a pale Stetson resting on the stony ground. The tight space hampering their movements, she moved to stand before Oona and adjusted her hold accordingly. She carefully set her down, crouching beside her legs as Oona stretched them out, inhaling sharply.

Reaching out, Talissa picked up the hat, briefly studying it before turning her attention back to Oona. 'We fetch Ecke,' she stated. 'You rest,' she added.

She nodded, leaning back against the cold stone. Her lids heavy, she stared up at Talissa, the branches beyond waving slightly in the wind. 'My thanks,' she croaked.

'We must go.' She sidled past Oona and climbed over the boulder that formed the head of the cleft, still holding onto the hat.

Making her way to her sister, she took Mausi's hand. Leading her to the path that climbed up beside The Overlook, the sisters made their way from the bank, taking the basket of washing with them.

42

A bed of rocks rested between Fitch and the fast flowing waters of the creek as he approached the waterfall. He moved along the bank, spying The Overlook before he reached the cliff. He saw no trace of Wallace or the horses and his expression became one of puzzlement.

'Where have you gone?' he whispered as he drew up to the edge, reaching out to hold onto the trunk of a sapling, some of its roots hanging out of the cliff below.

Surveying the area for a suitable place to descend, he saw a section that had caved in to his right and moved away from the creek. Passing through the trees as rain began to fall once more, he reached the fallen rocks and carefully made his way down.

Arriving at the bottom of the rough slope, he brushed off his hands and looked through the trees to The Overlook. Shaking his head, irritated by his partner's absence, he made his way towards the plateaux.

He came to a stop at its periphery, looking at the earth by his feet. Crouching, he stared at the diluted blood on the ground with an expression of confusion.

Absently scratching his beard and taking hold of his necklace as he thought, Fitch lifted his gaze. He saw drag marks in the grass and got to his feet, following them to the edge of The Overlook.

'If my guess is right, someone was thrown over,' he mumbled, reaching inside his coat for the tobacco, but his hand withdrawing when he recalled the state of his matches.

Grinding his teeth and feeling tightness in his brow due to his lack of nicotine, he stood and stared down at the pool. Looking downstream, he spied something bobbing in the water thirty yards away, snagged on an overhanging branch that dipped below the surface.

'Could be the nigger. Could be Wallace,' he stated, 'or could just be the litter of the forest.'

Turning and making his way to the trees, he noted hoof prints entering the forest. 'Maybe he went back to the cottage to wait,' he said doubtfully.

Fitch moved between the trunks, following the course of the creek. Gauging that he was near level with whatever was snagged in the water, he made towards it with purpose.

Reaching the bank, he peered across, his teeth creaking against each other as he continued to grind them. A small island of debris had become trapped against the branch. Something pale caught his eye amidst the detritus, but the reflection of the trees on the far bank obscured the sight.

He crouched to gain a better vantage point. Wallace's sightless eyes stared back at him from beneath the debris. His pale face was masked with bands of weed, but the bullet hole in his cheek was still visible.

Fitch looked at his partner in surprise. 'What in Sam Hill is going on?'

Drawing his gun, he looked about the surrounding forest, made nervous by the macabre discovery. He listened intently, the sense that someone was watching him sending a tremor along his spine.

Sidling to the nearest tree, he peered from behind, searching for any hint of anyone within the woodland. Seeing nothing, he shook his head and attempted to settle his rattled nerves.

'Pull yourself together,' he murmured, reprimanding himself and moving out from behind the tree.

He slipped the gun back in place and glanced at the creek as he began to walk away.

'Fuck!' he exclaimed as realisation dawned.

He returned to the bank and looked out across the water. 'The damn money,' he cursed.

'The nigger is sure gonna to pay for this,' he stated, taking off his jacket.

Hanging it from a branch, Fitch crouched and took off his boots and socks. Undoing his gun belt, he lay it over his boots and took off the rest of his clothing.

Naked by the creek, the bounty hunter took his gun and climbed gingerly into the water. Keeping a watchful eye on both banks, he waded towards the far side, the water reaching his ribcage at its deepest and the current pulling at him.

Taking hold of the overhanging branch upon which the debris was caught, he reached beneath the surface with his free hand. Grabbing hold of the coarse material of his partner's jacket, he gave it a hard yank.

Wallace's body came free, rising to the surface and rolling onto its back. The jacket was open, the sides drooping into the water to either side.

Awkwardly taking hold of his partner's shirt collar with his gun hand, Fitch reached for the right lapel with the other. He lifted the front pocket from the creek, already guessing at its emptiness due to the lack of weight.

Delving inside, he found the payment gone. He checked the inside pocket and the pockets of Wallace's britches, finding them equally as vacant. Cursing under his breath, he released the body, momentarily watching it float downstream.

Making his way back to the western bank, he drew himself out of the water with revolver held at the ready. Looking around before setting to the task of dressing, he placed the pistol within easy reach and donned his clothes, pale shirt sticking to his damp skin.

'He could've put the money in his saddlebag,' he said as he fastened his gun belt and took his jacket from the branch. Putting it on, he set off towards The Overlook, intent upon following the horses' tracks.

43

Oona listened as the bounty hunter undressed, still seated as Talissa had left her and body filled with torment. She'd been close to sleep, his loud curse causing her eyes to snap open and alerting her to his presence. The top of his head was visible above the rocks that formed the far end of the cleft, but she didn't try to rise in order to gain a better view, fear and lack of strength keeping her in place.

Her pulse increased as she heard him traverse the rocks. Worried that he was making his way towards her position, she looked up over her shoulder. The slope of the boulder at her back was beyond her ability to climb, her condition so poor that she was unable to flee.

Hearing the splash of water to her left, she turned to a crack between the rocks. Heart tumultuous, she stared without blinking as the bounty hunter came into sight, wading through the waters with gun in hand.

Her view limited by the narrow fissure, she saw him come to a halt and tug at something beneath the surface. Shock registered as the body floated into view.

Only able to see its torso, she looked on as Fitch searched the pockets. He released the corpse, his agitated expression reflected in the manner by which he began to make his way back to the shore.

He vanished from view and she listened as he exited the water and made his way back over the rocks to the bank. A few mumbled words were spoken, but she couldn't make them out as she took wavering breaths and hunkered down for fear of being discovered.

Fitch appeared on the bank above her position, fully dressed and with a purposeful stride. She held her breath, eyes wide as she stared at him through the branches veiling the cleft, praying that he wouldn't turn his gaze to the creek.

He vanished from sight and Oona exhaled. Gooseflesh rose on her skin and shivering took hold. She listened for any sign of his whereabouts, but the noises of the creek and forest hid any clue.

Her teeth began to chatter and she clenched her jaw to stop the sound, worried that he would hear it. Wrapping her arms about herself, she tried to find some small warmth, but all trace had vacated her. She imagined the life of her body retreating, its light drawing inward until its final flame was extinguished from her heart.

'Be this how I pay for my sin?' she asked, looking up through the branches, the harshness of the boulder against the back of her head.

Rain began to fall once again; at first only an irregular tapping upon the stones, but soon building into a cacophony of pattering droplets.

Keeping her face raised, Oona closed her eyes and let the drops fall upon her cheeks. 'A life for a life,' she whispered, the purity of heaven's tears upon her lips.

44

Ezra ducked out of sight behind a growth of ferns. Looking through the fronds, he watched as three natives passed, heading in the direction of the waterfall. One was a woman, her hands being held by two girls that he guessed to be her daughters. The eldest was leading the way, pulling her mother forward with urgency.

Waiting until they were gone, he rose and stared after them. 'Pa said there were still Injuns deep in the forest,' he commented, recalling his attempts to persuade his parents to give up their life in the wilderness after he'd been told of the natives.

He returned his attention to the trail he was following. Setting off, he remained alert, taking additional care to make as little noise as possible.

Soon after seeing the Indians, Ezra came to halt. Staring down at the hoof marks, he noted the evidence of further disturbance beside.

'Someone else found them first,' he whispered, the trail abruptly turning north, indicating that the horses were being led.

He began to follow, regularly glancing up to check for any sign of the beasts between the widely spaced trees ahead. Drops of rain fell from the branches, patting on the needles as he slipped his hand into his pocket and took hold of the gun. The memory of the tussle with the stranger came to the fore of his mind, his stomach churning in response.

Ezra tried to dispel the images and took a deep breath. He caught the smell of wood smoke on the wind and his brow became furrowed. His parents hadn't mentioned settlers and most of the gold mining was located further north along the Chattahoochee and Etowah rivers.

'The Injuns or maybe prospectors?' he muttered, continuing to follow the tracks.

He'd only been walking a short while when a scattering of huts arranged around a central building came into view fifty yards ahead. Ezra drew up behind a trunk and peered at the Creek settlement, seeing a number of the residents going about their daily routines. A pair of horses stood outside the main hut. He could make out the indents of where saddles had recently rested upon their backs and guessed they were the beasts he'd seen on The Overlook.

He crouched and leant against the pine as he tried to figure out the best course of action. He could pretend to be the owner, but how would he explain that both horses were saddled.

'My partner could be waiting for me at The Overlook,' he whispered, taking his cue from his chance meeting with Wallace.

He straightened and stepped from his concealment. Trying to adopt a confident stride, he made his way towards the huts, two of the women noting his approach as they exited the main building. They came to a stop and the nearest called over her shoulder. Four men soon joined them, two clutching spears and the others with weapons fashioned from large bones.

Ezra's pace slowed as they came towards him. Their expressions lacked friendliness and they gripped their weapons tightly, unveiled suspicion in their dark eyes.

'What you want?' asked Yaholo, gripping a spear and aiming its point directly at Ezra's chest as the group halted before him.

Ezra came to a stop. 'Those are my horses,' he said, pointing with his left hand as he continued to hold the gun hidden in his pocket.

Yaholo glanced back. 'They are two, you are one.'

'I have a partner. He is waiting by the creek for my return.'

'You lie. These horses were here with other men,' he stated, one of his companions nodding. 'They not yours.'

Ezra was caught off guard by the unexpected response. 'I…' He struggled to arrive at a suitable reply. 'I have two partners.'

'Leave,' ordered Yaholo, prodding the air with his spear.

He looked at the faces of the Creek as he considered what to do. 'My parents,' he began, deciding to tell them the truth and appeal to their compassion. 'They lived in a cottage to the south. They had tables for birds and other animals. Did you know them?'

Yaholo glanced at his companions. 'We know of who you speak.'

'They were killed yesterday,' stated Ezra. 'I believe those horses might belong to the men who murdered them. Will you let me look in the saddlebags?'

Yaholo looked to the man beside him who had been present when Wallace and Fitch had come searching for the runaway. They spoke a few words in their native language and he turned his attention back to Ezra.

'You know these men?' he asked.

Ezra shook his head.

'They look for a nigger girl.'

The image of the small sleeping space beside the chimney arose in Ezra's mind. 'A nigger girl?'

Yaholo nodded.

'Did they mention where they'd been before coming to you?'

'They only say they look.'

'Can I see their bags?'

Yaholo pondered, looking to the ground. 'You have weapon?' he asked after a moment.

'Just this.' Ezra slowly withdrew the gun from his pocket, letting it rest upon his palm.

'You give it, you look in bags.'

He looked at the revolver, wary of handing over his only means of protection and yet relieved that he was to be rid of the weapon. It was a reminder of what had happened and evidence of his involvement in Wallace's accidental death.

Holding it out to the Creek, Yaholo walked forward and took it from him. Examining it and checking the chamber, he tucked it into his loincloth.

'Follow,' he instructed, turning and walking towards the central hut, the other three men parting to allow him to pass.

Ezra looked at them nervously and began to follow. They fell into step behind him and his tension increased.

'Was there a crossbow on the horses?' he asked, the thought coming to mind and glad for the distraction from the potential danger at his back.

Yaholo simply shook his head as he neared the main hut, the women still standing near its entrance taking a few steps back. Reaching for the skin that hung over the doorway, he made to enter, placing his hand to the edge in readiness to draw it back. Ezra went towards it, but the Creek leader placed his hand to his chest, stopping him in his tracks.

'It is forbidden,' he stated. 'I fetch bags.' He pulled back the skin and slipped inside.

Ezra stood and waited, the presence of the three Creek men very apparent and keeping him on edge.

There was talking inside the main hut, Yaholo's voice joined by that of an old man.

He reappeared carrying saddlebags. Taking a couple of steps away from the entrance, he placed them on the ground as an elderly Creek exited and studied Ezra, eyes milky and nestled within a multitude of crow's feet.

'Look,' said Yaholo, indicating the bags.

Ezra went over to them and settled upon his haunches. Searching through them one at a time, he came upon a sheaf of papers and slipped them out. Leafing through them, he looked for anything that may hint that the men had been responsible for the death of his parents.

'Handbills,' he said to himself, finding that most related to slaves that had run away from plantations and the like.

He went still when he reached the last. It was a letter addressed to Mr Wallace. The image of the slumped body haunted him as he read the correspondence. It spoke of a thirteen year old slave that had taken a razor to her master's throat. She'd run and eluded those who'd given chase. The letter offered a fee for locating and detaining her, and had been written by the brother of the deceased, one Mr J. Woodruff.

Ezra's belief that the slave must have been abiding at the cottage was strengthened. He knew of his parents' unnatural attitude towards the coloureds, that they were likely to have taken such a stray into their home.

He shook his head and took a deep breath. 'A nigger brought about their end,' he stated.

Sliding the other papers back into the bag, he got to his feet. 'I keep this one,' he said, holding it up.

Yaholo glanced at the elderly Mico, who nodded his acquiescence.

'You take,' he agreed.

169

'Much obliged,' replied Ezra, folding the letter along the creases which already ran the width of the page and slipping it into the inside pocket of his jacket.

45

She woke to her shoulder being shaken. Wearily opening her eyes, Oona found Talissa looking down at her in concern, the rain having ceased once more.

'I bring Ecke,' she stated, looking over Oona.

She turned her head, finding Talissa's mother and sister staring down from the top of the boulder against which she was leaning.

'We get you to village.'

'No!' Her mother's response was immediate and sharp.

Talissa looked at her in surprise.

Cocheta said a few native words.

'English, so she know what we speak,' insisted Talissa with a glance towards Oona.

Cocheta stared at her, sighing when she recognised the determination which had passed down through their female ancestors for generations. 'We treat here,' she stated, reiterating what she'd already said in Muskogean.

'Why not take to our hut, give shelter and food?'

'No outsiders,' replied her mother.

'She have need.' Talissa held her hands out towards Oona.

'We treat here,' restated Cocheta.

They held each other's gaze for a moment. Seeing that her mother would not change her mind, Talissa looked down at the slave girl regretfully.

'We treat you here. I bring skins later and make good this shelter,' she said without glancing at her mother, knowing that she would be expressing disapproval.

Crouching by Oona's legs, she lifted the hem of the slave's sodden housedress and looked at the damaged knee. It was bruised and swollen. 'Broken?' she asked her mother.

'Move back,' said Cocheta.

Talissa stood and moved to the far end of the cleft. Her mother slipped down the near side of the boulder, careful not to knock into Oona.

Moving to her side, she settled and reached towards the knee. 'Will hurt,' she said with a quick glance.

She felt the joint, her touch without tenderness. Oona winced and inhaled sharply as pain flared.

'Not broken,' stated Cocheta as she withdrew her hand. 'Need rest and time,' she added, looking to cuts and bruising on Oona's arms. 'You have more?'

Oona nodded. 'On my side and shins,' she replied, shifting with discomfort.

Cocheta took a folded leaf from a pouch at the front of her hide dress. Opening it, she revealed a green paste contained within. She held it out to Talissa. 'Put on cuts.'

Talissa took it from her mother.

'I take Mausi back. You come when done.'

'You go?'

'Nothing more to do.'

Talissa frowned, but did not argue.

'You come soon,' said Cocheta, moving to the boulder at the head of the cleft and making her way over it.

'My thanks,' said Oona groggily.

Nodding and taking her youngest daughter's hand, Cocheta began to make her way towards the patch of bank beside The Overlook. Mausi tried to linger, looking back over her shoulder. Cocheta scolded her in their native tongue, all but dragging the girl in her wake.

'Good for cuts,' said Talissa, taking some of the paste onto her index and middle fingers.

Oona braced herself for pain as the native girl began to apply it to the cuts. To her surprise, the paste bore no sting, but was cool and soothing, reminding her of the curative which Dorothy had made. Relaxing against the boulder, Talissa attentively tended the visible wounds on her arms and legs.

'You want I do cuts on side?' she asked once finished.

Oona shook her head, rubbing her arms as shivering returned.

'You do?'

She gave a nod of response. 'I do,' she confirmed, trying to control the quaking of her body as exposure began to take its toll.

Talissa studied her a moment. 'Why you in water?'

Oona looked into her inquisitive eyes. 'I done fell in when trying to cross the creek.'

'The men who come to village,' stated Talissa. 'They ask for you. Why?'

'I…' She looked down. 'I ran away.'

'Why you run away?'

Oona's eyes welled with tears. She shook her head, throat and chest tightening.

Seeing her distress, Talissa reached out and placed her hand upon her shoulder. 'You had good reason.'

'Yes,' she whispered, 'but there be more.'

Oona raised her glistening eyes. 'I be a killer.'

Talissa removed her hand, resting back on her haunches as she regarded Oona with disbelief. 'You play?'

Oona shook her head. 'It be the truth.'

'Who you kill?' asked Talissa, still unsure as to the honesty of Oona's testament.

'My master. All this…' She looked down at her battered body, '…be my punishment.'

173

Talissa stared at Oona thoughtfully. 'He a good man?'

'No.'

She took hold of Oona's hand and lifted it, looking at the scars about her wrist. 'Treat you bad?'

'Yes, and he done killed my friend,' replied Oona, the image of Etty's beaten and bloody countenance coming to mind.

'Maybe you his punishment,' suggested Talissa, gently setting the slave's hand back upon her lap.

Oona shook her head. 'I be a bad person. I be sinful.'

Talissa stared at her, seeing the tears in her eyes and tormented expression. 'Bad person not feel as you. Bad person not care.'

'But I done committed a great sin.'

'Cehecis,' said Talissa, unintentionally slipping into Muskogean. 'You not bad person.'

'Cehecis?' asked Oona.

'Mean, "I see you",' replied Talissa.

Oona tried to think on what had been said, but was unable to grasp onto the words, her mind befuddled. She held herself tightly, gritting her teeth against the shivering that had overtaken her.

'You need fire,' stated Talissa with concern. 'I take you to village.'

'Your mother…'

Talissa held up her hand. 'I not leave you like this.'

She moved to sit in front of Oona and held out her hand. 'I get you there.'

Oona took hold. Talissa pulled, arms and shoulders straining as Oona did her best to rise, unable to put much pressure on her injured knee. Managing to get to her feet, she almost collapsed forward, the Creek girl taking her into her arms and staggering back under the weight.

Moving to stand beside Oona once her balance was regained, she put her arm about her. 'Together,' she stated, nodding towards the head of the cleft.

One step at a time, they moved through the narrow space to the boulder against which Oona had been leaning. Talissa released her hold and climbed up, perching at the top.

Holding out her hand, Oona took it and was helped up. She inhaled sharply between her teeth when her knee clashed with the stone, her grip on Talissa's hand tightening.

Making the climb, she slid forward once over the top, bracing herself against other rocks with the palms of her hands. Talissa helped right her, both girls putting all their effort into getting Oona back on her feet.

They awkwardly made their way towards the bank. Teetering and needing to reach out to nearby boulders, the passage through the shoreline rocks was arduous. Oona continued to shiver despite the perspiration building on her body, adding to the dampness already present after the rain.

Reaching the trees, they found the going easier, the rocks breaking and earth taking their place. Arm around Oona, Talissa was breathless and thankful to be leaving the creek behind. She glanced at the slave, seeing the strain in the tightness of her expression as she limped along with her support.

Oona stumbled, her legs lacking coordination and feeling drowsy. 'I need to rest,' she mumbled, mouth thick with phlegm.

'You rest at village,' responded Talissa. 'You need dry and warm.'

Oona hadn't the energy to protest. She tried to focus her sluggish thoughts on each movement, feet heavy upon the mat of needles and toes dragging with each forward step. The pain in her knee lurked in the back of her mind, masked by her failing condition as they slowly passed through the trees and the clouds above began to break.

46

Ezra walked away from the settlement, shoulders tense as the Creek villagers watched him leave. He glanced back nervously, finding them attentive to his every move.

Retreating further into the trees, his thoughts turned to his next course of action. He wasn't prepared to head back to his parents' cottage without finding out the truth about their deaths, so only one option remained open to him; to find Wallace's partner.

'He said he was waiting for him at The Overlook,' he mumbled, looking over his shoulder and seeing that the village was hidden from sight by the trees.

'Stop right there.'

Ezra turned back to the direction of travel, coming face to face with a bearded man who'd stepped from behind a large pine. His gaze immediately settled on the crossbow in the man's hands, bolt aimed at his chest.

'Where'd you get that?' he asked, noting the lines etched into the wood which marked how many squirrels his father had shot.

'Why was you talking with those Injuns?' Fitch glared at him, crossbow steady.

Ezra held his gaze. 'You killed my parents,' he stated.

The bounty hunter looked at him in confusion. 'The couple at the shack? Ain't no better way for nigger lovers to go.'

Ezra made to step towards him and he raised the crossbow.

'Now, now. You don't want to be ending up the same way, do you?'

'You son of a bitch!' hissed Ezra, becoming stationary.

'That's me,' said Fitch, grinning nastily. 'For better or for worse, as they say.'

He took a step back. 'What was you talking to the Injuns about?'

'I'm not telling you a goddamn thing,' replied Ezra.

'Maybe if I skewer you, it'll loosen your tongue,' he pointed the bow at Ezra's leg and pulled the trigger.

The bolt flew free, embedding itself in Ezra's thigh. Letting out a yell of pain, he fell to his knees.

Fitch put the head of the crossbow to the ground and quickly reloaded it with the last remaining bolt before looming over his victim. Ezra squirmed, features made tight by agony.

'HELP ME!' he yelled, straining his neck to look towards the settlement. 'HELP…'

Fitch kicked him in the side, knocking the air from his lungs and sending him tumbling over. 'Shut up or I'll be shutting you up,' he warned. 'I'll ask you again; what was you doing with those Injuns?'

'Checking your saddlebags.' His voice was strained as he stared up at the bounty hunter.

'For what?'

'To see if you were responsible for killing my parents.'

'Well, now you know. Can't see that there's much you can do about it though,' he said with a sneer. 'You ain't got too long until you bleed out.'

Ezra looked down at his leg, seeing the blood soaking his britches and dripping to the pine needles.

'I could put you out of your misery, I suppose,' suggested Fitch, pointing the bolt at his forehead, 'but that depends on what you can tell me about my partner.'

Ezra looked up at his assailant as he decided whether or not to reveal the truth. 'It was an accident.'

'It was you!' Fitch's smile vanished in an instant and he pushed the tip of the bolt to Ezra's forehead. 'Where's the money?'

'Money?'

'The payment for finding the nigger gal.'

Ezra thought for a moment. 'Maybe in your saddlebags. The Injuns have them.'

Fitch glanced in the direction of the Creek village.

Ezra reached up and tried to bat the crossbow away.

The bounty hunter looked down at him and shook his head. 'That weren't a wise move,' he stated, increasing the pressure on the trigger.

47

Oona and Talissa made their way to the settlement with increasing difficulty. The creek had fallen away behind them, its burbling replaced by birdsong and the whispering of the trees. A squirrel leapt from branch to branch, pausing to look down upon the weary figures.

Oona's head hung low and her body sagged under the weight of her weariness. She hobbled as best she could, her good foot dragging and scuffing the ground.

Her arm and shoulder aching, Talissa gritted her teeth. Oona was leaning on her with growing need, borrowing momentum from the native girl in order to continue.

'How far?' asked Oona.

'Close,' replied Talissa, wiping her brow with the back of her free hand.

'Good.' Oona gave a shallow nod.

Talissa looked at her fretfully. Her condition had worsened considerably during the journey. She wondered if she'd done the right thing in bringing her from the cleft, if it wouldn't have been better to leave her there in order to rest and regain some of her stamina.

'You hear?' she asked, scanning the trees after thinking she heard a cry on the wind.

'Hear what?' Oona turned to her with hooded eyes.

'Someone call out,' replied Talissa as she brought them to a halt, grateful for the respite.

Oona cocked her head and listened, hearing nothing untoward. 'I don't hear anyone.'

Talissa's brow creased as she continued to glance around, the muffled sound having no clear direction of origin. 'It sound like a man, a man in trouble.'

'One of your people?'

Talissa shrugged. 'Could be.'

Hearing nothing more, she looked to Oona. 'Ready?'

She nodded weakly.

They set off, Oona barely able to remain on her feet. Their pace was ponderous, footsteps irregular and heavy.

48

Fitch stood over Ezra with crossbow in hand. Hearing evidence of movement behind him, he quickly turned, fearful that natives from the settlement had heard Ezra's plea and were coming to investigate.

His gaze fell upon Oona and Talissa as they passed through the trees thirty yards away. Neither had noticed his presence, too intent on reaching the settlement.

'Looks like I've found what I've been looking for,' he said under his breath, his grin returning.

Ezra saw the girls and turned back to Fitch, seeing him reach for the gun at his hip.

'RUN!' he yelled.

The girls turned to the warning. Surprise registered in their expressions as they set eyes on the two men.

Fitch drew his pistol, keeping the crossbow aimed at Ezra as he remained upon the ground by his feet. 'Oona Mae,' he called, pointing the gun at the girls. 'I've been looking for you.'

Talissa glanced at Oona, seeing terror in her dark eyes. 'The trunk,' she whispered, nodding towards a pine only a few steps ahead.

They moved towards the tree and all but fell behind its protection, scrambling back against the bark, shoulder to shoulder. Satisfied that Ezra wouldn't be able to make an escape due to the bolt through his leg, Fitch stalked towards them, seeing the edge of Oona's housedress.

'What do we do?' asked Oona, her weariness chased away by the adrenalin of panic.

Talissa looked in the direction of the village. 'I run for help.'

'But he's got a gun.'

'I run,' she reiterated readying herself to sprint from cover.

She leapt up and set off.

A gunshot cracked through the forest.

Talissa's legs gave way and she careened headlong into the ground. Her hands out before her, a shower of earth and pine needles was sent into the air.

'NO!' shouted Oona as she looked to the native girl, who was writhing in pain, the bullet having torn through her calf.

She grasped the tree and hauled herself up. Stumbling towards Talissa, she glanced to the left and saw Fitch approaching, a thin tongue of smoke rising from the pistol in his hand.

Oona fell beside Talissa, her back to the bounty hunter. Taking the native girl in her arms, she shielded her with her body.

Fitch came to halt beside them. 'Ain't that grand; a nigger girl protecting a no good savage,' he sneered.

Bending, he grasped Oona's hair. He tugged and she was forced to release Talissa as she was brought unwillingly to her feet.

Fitch raised his hand to such a height that Oona had to stand on tiptoes, her eyes watering. He stared at the young girl before him dispassionately. 'Good teeth,' he observed with a wicked glint in his eyes.

There was a sound like a breath of wind. The tip of a spear burst from Fitch's chest, stopping a mere inch from Oona's throat. He stared down at it in shock as she looked over his shoulder to see four Creek men running towards them.

Fitch released his hold and she collapsed to the ground. Turning, he aimed the revolver at Yaholo, who was sprinting at the head of the group.

Seeing what he was about to do, Oona jumped up. Using her last reserves of strength, she dived between the bounty hunter and his intended victim.

Fitch fired.

Agony filled Oona's chest as she fell to the ground and one of the Creek men accompanying Yaholo threw his spear. She lay breathless and body trembling as the weapon buried its shaft deep in Fitch's chest.

He looked at the two spears embedded in his torso, blood seeping from the corners of his mouth. Gun falling from his grasp, he toppled forwards. Twitching momentarily, his body fell still.

Talissa crawled towards Oona, nails digging into the soil. She reached the slave girl as her father and his companions came to a halt beside. Turning her over, she heaved Oona's head onto her lap.

'Oona?' she said, face reddened by the pain of her injury.

The girl's eyelids flickered, opening a little. She looked up at the four Creek men, a faint smile upon her lips. 'They be unharmed,' she breathed. 'Are you badly hurt?' she asked, turning her gaze to Talissa.

She shook her head. 'You save Father,' she stated.

'I'm glad,' responded Oona. 'No one else must die for me.'

She coughed and a touch of blood coloured her lips.

Talissa looked up at her father questioningly. Yaholo shook his head and she bit back tears.

'It be all right,' said Oona, her fingers flexing with the wish to grasp Talissa's hand, but arm to heavy to lift.

Her eyes briefly rolled back as she struggled to remain conscious. 'I can hear the birds singing,' she said with a pained smile. 'It be like they sing for me.'

She coughed and momentarily winced with pain. Her sight went in and out of focus as she tried to make out Talissa's face. 'For I'll be coming home,' she whispered.

She closed her eyes and her breathing shallowed. Talissa looked upon her helplessly, noting the blood seeping through the dishevelled pinafore covering Oona's housedress.

She inhaled deeply, chest expanding. Her final breath was soft and long, taken by the breeze and woven through the trees.

As her body relaxed and the tension in her face fell away, a beam of sunlight broke through the clouds. Piercing the forest canopy, it rested upon her head, her hair a dark halo glistening with moisture.

At the age of thirteen, Oona found redemption.

Epilogue

Yaholo helped Ezra onto his horse, which had been recovered from the forest four days prior. He settled in the saddle with a groan, his leg bandaged and the wound healed enough for him to make the journey back to Johanna and his children.

Most of the village were gathered to watch his departure, the main building at their backs. Talissa and Mausi stood with their mother near the front of the group, the sisters holding hands.

'Thank you,' he said, cheeks flushed by the effort.

'Journey safe,' replied Yaholo.

Ezra nodded, taking up the reins and nudging his mount in the flanks. It set off at its usual plodding pace and he turned it southward, his back to the Creek as they looked on.

The crowd began to disperse as he moved through the pines and disappeared from view. Talissa and Mausi were the last to remain, their mother drifting off with a couple of the other women, the three of them conversing in hushed tones.

Unable to see any trace of Ezra, the two girls turned and headed east, their hands staying linked. The trees were without whispering, the day bright and still. Birds sang and flitted amidst the boughs, flashes of gold, red and blue.

The creek came into earshot before it could be seen, its waters calling the girls onward. Their leisurely pace was quickened by the proximity of their destination and The Overlook came into view between the trunks.

They paused at its edge, both turning to the grave at the northern side of the outcrop. It was no more than a heap of stones, a few wildflowers already showing between.

Talissa led them over to stand at its foot. 'Oona,' she whispered, bowing in greeting.

A swallowtail butterfly settled on Mausi's shoulder and flexed its wings in the sunshine. She turned to its surprising presence and the insect lifted into the air gracefully. It fluttered to the grave, landing on a flower with yellow petals near the centre. Finding pollen, it sat with wings open as it had its fill and then took to the wing, circling before passing over the edge of The Overlook.

Talissa smiled. 'Now you free.'

Afterward

After taking a break from writing tales relating to slavery in order to write a historical superhero novel set in 1910/11 London (entitled *Rise of Ox* and due for release late in 2019), it was a pleasure to return to the subject in order to tell Oona's story. I soon became fond of her and was gladdened when she found moments of happiness with Dorothy and Walter.

There were a number of surprises for me while writing the book, some of which will have also been surprises for you. The most prominent in my mind is when Oona tumbles into the creek when crossing the fallen pine. I had not anticipated this turn of events and it went on to change what happened for the remainder of the book. If she hadn't fallen in, she would not have been hurt when caught by the current. She also wouldn't have been rescued by Talissa and placed in the cleft of rock. Most of the final portion of the story was moulded by her fall and yet I had no idea it was going to happen.

When I first began writing this book, I thought the first chapter would be a prologue and the second would see Oona a few years older and living wild in the forest. I had no idea that she did not live to see fourteen, at least, not in the sense that we regard as living. As it was, she knew her story, whereas I was merely relating her words and deeds.

As for the words used by the Creek, they are of the Muskogean language, which was commonly used by a number of tribes. Most are translated within the story, with the exception of Mico, which was the name for the chief of a town. It may be that the word 'Cehecis,' meaning 'I see you,' inspired the relevant content in the movie *Avatar*. It is also pertinent to mention that there is another Muskogean word that means 'you see me,' and this is 'Cvhecetskes.'

All of the Creek names used have meanings. These are as follows:

Talissa (usually spelt with only one 's'): Beautiful Water

Mausi: Plucks Petals

Cocheta: Stranger

Yaholo: One Who Shouts

Finally, I think it's important to say that the process of writing fiction does not just happen when I'm typing. When I'm not at my laptop, there is still activity in both my conscious and subconscious. The conscious tends to remember things that I have forgotten to include while typing. These are usually small touches, like forgetting to include that Walter leaves his crossbow loaded when leant up. At the same time, the subconscious is creating what's to come. It is where Oona abided, living her story and passing it on to my conscious mind while typing. In tandem, they work together to deliver what I hope are satisfying tales.

Historical Facts Relevant to the Story:
1. The gold rush occurred in the late 1820s and by 1832 gold prospecting had expanded throughout the mountains of North Georgia.
2. Between 1832 and 1839, the Creek, Seminole, Cherokee, Chickasaw and Choctaw tribes were removed from their ancestral hunting grounds and forced to relocate to the Indian Territory. They were known as the Five Civilised Tribes and the journey to the Territory became known as the Trail of Tears.

3. A surveyor in Michigan is thought to be the possible origin of the phrase 'Sam Hill.' Samuel W. Hill lived from 1819 to 1889 and supposedly used such foul language that his name became a euphemism for curse words.

Thank you for reading this book and I hope it touched your heart.

Publisher's Note: Edwin Page's tenth story relating to slavery will be released on July 1st 2019. Entitled *Pine Ridge*, it tells the story of a couple who purchase a plantation house in present day Alabama, but the past soon comes back to haunt them.

CPSIA information can be obtained
at www.ICGtesting.com
Printed in the USA
LVHW031021230320
650895LV00007B/2076

9 781092 168526